First Response in Florida

Bachelor brothers and passionate protectors!

Adopted brothers Jackson and Luis are exactly
the men you want in a crisis—tall, strong…
and incredibly handsome! Not to mention their
guarded hearts of gold. And when an inbound
tropical storm threatens the Florida Keys,
these medics are the first to become part of
the response team.

No one said that it would be easy, and leading
a team of dedicated volunteers is going to
test them to their limits. But they're certainly
up to the task. It's being caught in the eye of a
very different kind of storm that they have to
worry about… One where passion is the
key to survival!

Discover Jackson and Lucy's story in
The Vet's Unexpected Hero

And read Luis and Stacy's story in
Her One-Night Secret

Both available now!

Dear Reader,

Book two in my First Response in Florida duet features Dr. Luis Durand, the second of two adopted brothers who live and work in Key West, Florida. This book's full of secrets, along with lots of heart-pounding action and suspense as Hurricane Mathilda arrives on the doorstep!

Luis is a man on a mission. Given that his birth parents died trying to escape Cuba to give him a better life, Luis had always felt the weight of that sacrifice heavily and has been determined to live his life in service to others, even if it means putting his own personal relationships on the back burner. The only time he threw caution to the wind was four years prior when he had a one-night stand before leaving for an overseas humanitarian mission. Memories of that night, and the woman he left behind—firefighter Stacy Williams— have stayed with him, but he's about to discover something even more precious remains from that brief fling...

Will these two strong, stubborn spirits find their way to happily-ever-after even as the world around them is thrown into dangerous chaos by the storm?

You'll have to read their story to find out!

Traci

HER ONE-NIGHT
SECRET

———

TRACI DOUGLASS

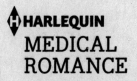

HARLEQUIN
MEDICAL
ROMANCE

HARLEQUIN®
MEDICAL ROMANCE™

Recycling programs
for this product may
not exist in your area.

ISBN-13: 978-1-335-40455-8

Her One-Night Secret

Copyright © 2021 by Traci Douglass

Harlequin Enterprises ULC
22 Adelaide St. West, 40th Floor
Toronto, Ontario M5H 4E3, Canada
www.Harlequin.com

Printed in U.S.A.

Traci Douglass is a *USA TODAY* bestselling author of contemporary and paranormal romance. Her stories feature sizzling heroes full of dark humor, quick wit and major attitude, and heroines who are smart, tenacious and always give as good as they get. She holds an MFA in Writing Popular Fiction from Seton Hill University, and she loves animals, chocolate, coffee, hot British actors and sarcasm— not necessarily in that order.

Books by Traci Douglass

Harlequin Medical Romance

First Response in Florida
The Vet's Unexpected Hero

One Night with the Army Doc
Finding Her Forever Family
A Mistletoe Kiss for the Single Dad
A Weekend with Her Fake Fiancé
Their Hot Hawaiian Fling

Visit the Author Profile page at Harlequin.com.

Praise for
Traci Douglass

"*Their Hot Hawaiian Fling* by Traci Douglass is a fantastic romance.... I love this author's medical romance books and this is no exception. Both characters are well written, complex, flawed and well fleshed out. The story was perfectly paced. A great romance I highly recommend."

—*Goodreads*

CHAPTER ONE

Fɪʀᴇ Cᴀᴘᴛᴀɪɴ Sᴛᴀᴄʏ Wɪʟʟɪᴀᴍs climbed out of the back of the fire truck just as soon as it halted beneath the ambulance bay of Key West General Hospital, along with most of the rescue crew. They'd only left a skeleton staff back at the firehouse in case of other emergency calls coming in, as per protocol. Everyone else was here because one of their own was on a stretcher today.

She trailed behind the EMTs wheeling in Assistant Chief Reed Parker, unable to look away from Reed's too-pale face. The guy had been with the department for more than two decades, dedicating his life to protecting the good people of Key West, but today the father of three was the one who needed saving.

"What's the rundown?" one of the ER docs said as they lowered the gurney from the back of the ambulance. Stacy's focus remained steady on Reed, not looking up or budging as noise from the controlled chaos of the busy trauma department inside leaked out each time the automatic doors whooshed open then closed.

"Forty-one-year-old firefighter with Key West FD," one of the EMTs, Jackson Durand, said. "Riding his motorcycle and thrown from the bike, no loss of consciousness on scene. Obvious open left femur fracture."

Reed moaned loudly then and tried to get up, but Jackson held him in place with a hand on his chest. Stacy's heart went out to the guy. Reed prized his bike and rode to escape the stress of the job. To have this happen doing something he loved was devastating. They all clambered inside then down a corridor to the left toward one of the open treatment bays.

"Sir," the ER doc said, leaning over Reed as he stepped in beside Jackson, his back to Stacy. "Can you tell me your name?"

They transferred Reed from the gurney to the hospital bed, and one of the nurses lifted the sheet covering his lower body to look at the wound. "What's wrong with my leg?" he groaned, and Stacy's heart thudded hard in her chest. "It hurts so bad."

"Your leg is broken, sir," the doctor said,

placing his stethoscope on the man's chest and listening before continuing. "Pretty badly, I'm afraid. But we're going to take good care of you." He nodded to Jackson, then took over the EMT's position at the patient's bedside. "Okay, we've got a good airway here. Good breath sounds bilaterally. Sir, can you open your eyes again for me? Looks like you're getting drowsy. Reed, can you wiggle your left toes for me?"

Reed screamed, writhing on the bed. "Argh! It hurts, it hurts. I can't. I can't. My leg hurts so bad."

"Blood pressure?" the doctor asked the nurse across the gurney.

"Seventy over forty, Doc."

Stacy stood with the rest of her crew in the hallway outside the treatment bay, close enough to hear what was being done and said but out of the way of the important staff. As the assessment of Reed's condition continued, her gut knotted tighter in empathy for her coworker. An open compound fracture of the femur would hurt like hell, yet the hospital wouldn't be able to give him anything for the pain because of his low blood pressure. It could lead to even more issues, maybe even kill him if Reed stopped breathing all together.

Not good. Not good at all.

"Right," the doctor said, his slight accent snagging something in Stacy's memory before she waved it off. Key West was a true melting pot of people, between the locals and the vacationers and the refugees who came here for a better life. Just because that deep voice reminded her of a long-ago night on the beach, when a handsome Cuban stranger had wooed her into one night of passion that led to her son, Miguel, didn't mean it was the same guy. Couldn't be. The man she'd known was halfway around the world by now, location unknown...

"Let's give him six units of blood, stat!" the doctor said from the treatment bay, jarring Stacy out of the past and back to the high-stakes reality. "Heart rate's high but blood pressure's low. Get ortho on the phone, stat, please. This man needs to be in an operating room now. I don't know if that leg is salvageable, but right now the primary concern is stopping the bleeding and saving his life."

Stacy stepped back, head lowered, as the curtain swished open and the doctor walked out. She caught a hint of alcohol from the hand sanitizer he used as he passed by her, his rubber soles squeaking on the shiny tile floor as he headed to the nurses' station down the hall. He was tall, maybe six inches above her own five-foot-six height, with broad shoulders that filled out his green scrubs nicely. She still had no idea what he looked like, though, since she hadn't seen his face. She and the rest of the crew knew most of the docs around here, as they often assisted the ambulance crews on emergency runs since they were cross-trained as EMTs. Most times, fire arrived before the ambulance when 911 was called.

One of the nurses she knew, Jenny, walked out of the treatment bay, and Stacy plied her for information about Reed while Jenny typed into a computer against the wall. "How is he?"

"Not good," Jenny said. "He's not responding to the blood we're giving him. Doc's sending him up to surgery to see what's happening internally. We'll know more after that."

Jenny took off again, and Stacy and the rest of her crew wandered back down the corridor toward the waiting area, passing by the doc on the phone as they went. She did her best not to eavesdrop, but given it was a friend of hers whose life was in peril, that was pretty much impossible. Stacy wasn't sure whom he was talking to, but she was able to glean a few more details as she passed by.

"...yes. Fireman thrown from his motorcycle. Known femur fracture, suspected pelvic fracture. No. I'm not sure, but he's not responding to transfusions. That's my worry, too. Maybe an undiagnosed solid organ injury. Liver or spleen. Or perhaps internal bleeding from the pelvic fracture. We can't be certain until you get in there. Saving the leg is the least of our worries..."

Oh boy. Stacy sat in one of the hard plastic chairs and stared down at her hands.

Please, God. Please let Reed be okay. Please.

She couldn't imagine having that conversation with his wife, his kids. Telling them their father had died. Images from her own childhood, the day her mother had told Stacy that her dad was gone, flashed in her head.

Her dad hadn't died. He'd just walked out on them, but still.

She'd never seen the man again either way, so it didn't much matter.

The doctor hung up, and Stacy pushed to her feet. Enough. She needed to find out what was happening before Reed's family showed up demanding answers. As captain and the ranking officer on scene, it would be her duty to keep the family and her team informed.

Before she could reach the doc, whose long legs carried him surprisingly fast toward the stairwell, the automatic doors swished open once more and Reed's wife, Annette, ran in with their three teenaged kids.

"What's happened? Where's my husband?" Annette said in a panicked rush. "Is he okay? I told him not to ride that damned bike of his so fast around the curves. I told him he was going to kill himself one day if he…" Her words caught on a sob, and she collapsed into Stacy's arms. "Oh God. I didn't mean it. I swear I didn't. If anything happens to my Reed, I don't know what I'll do."

Stacy led the crying woman and the kids to a more private area down the hall, near the elevators, to tell her what she knew, which was precious little at the moment until she talked to the doctor in charge. She looked up and spotted him still near the nurses' station, talking to Jackson. Good. Maybe if she hurried she could still catch him before he went up to surgery, or wherever he was going.

"Hang on, Annie," Stacy said, gripping the near-hysterical woman by the shoulders.

"Let me see if I can catch the doctor real quick and find out what's happening."

She looked up again and froze.

Not because the doctor was gone, but because she finally got a look at his face. A face she'd never thought she'd see again. She blinked, stared, the phantom smells of sand and surf surrounding her. The sounds of the ER morphed into the crash of waves. They'd been young and drunk and stupid in lust with each other, both looking for a good time, nothing more.

She'd ended up with more, though. A life-altering more that had given her more joy and sorrow and unexpected gifts that she'd ever imagined. A son she'd never expected. A son his father knew nothing about.

Oh no.

Her breath seized, and her chest ached. Time slowed as her eyes locked with his hazel ones, the same caramel color she remembered from that long-ago night on the beach.

It was him.

Luis.

Then, as quickly as the spell had fallen, it shattered, and things sped up. He pushed through the stairwell door and was gone, looking as shell-shocked as she felt. Stacy was left staring at Jackson, who gave her an inquiring look before going back to his paperwork.

Snap out of it, she scolded herself. *Breathe.*

She couldn't afford this right now. Not with Reed fighting for his life and an Emergency Response Team meeting on her agenda in a little over an hour's time.

Dammit. She was supposed to meet her friend Lucy Miller and take her to the meeting. It was Lucy's first time and she was anxious as it was, and Stacy didn't want to make that worse.

"Come on," she said to Annette, ushering her and the kids into a private consult room nearby. "You guys sit here for a little while until we find out more, okay?" She hugged Annie, then excused herself. "I'll be back. I need to take care of something." Stacy headed out the door then turned back to her crew, who were sitting with the Parkers. "Watch over them. Text me if anything changes."

Then she was out the door and heading for the waiting area where she was supposed to meet Lucy, but nope. No sign of her friend. Dammit. Stacy checked everywhere, even went up to the children's ward but found no Lucy or her service dog, Sam.

She went back to the nurses' station, thinking she'd ask Jackson, but he was gone now, too.

Great. Her day was going from bad to worse.

It can't be. And yet...it was.

He knew that as surely as he knew the patient he was watching through the glass of the observation room upstairs in the OR would still have a long way to go before he was out of the woods. The surgery could stop the bleeding and stabilize his condition. That was the good news. The bad news was afterward they'd still need to evaluate that leg, wash out the wound to get rid of all the gravel and denim and bits of bone that had been broken off and were embedded with it. Then the ortho surgeon would apply a fixation device to stabilize his broken femur. Unfortunately, when Luis had checked in the ER, there was no pulse in the patient's left foot, and from what he could hear through the intercom system from the surgical suite, there still wasn't now, even after an hour on the table. Which could signify two bigger injuries—compromised blood supply to the leg or possible nerve damage to the area.

Yes, the man's life was much more secure at that point, but at what cost?

It was a question that plagued Luis as he went back downstairs for the ERT meeting. He was already running late, which was nothing new. Schedules had to be flexible when you packed as much into them as Luis did. He liked to stay busy, stay productive, stay focused on his goals.

After all, people had died to make his life today possible. People like his birth parents.

He owed it to them to accomplish as much as possible for as many people as possible in the time he had. It was a philosophy that Luis lived by and the idea that kept him circling back to that original question, usually late at night, when he lay awake in his bed, alone.

At what cost?

Luis wasn't a man who sat around feeling sorry for himself. Nope. He was blessed, and he knew it.

He pushed out into the ER on the first floor and checked in at the nurses' station before grabbing his lab coat and heading down the hall to the conference room where the meeting was being held. He nodded greetings to several colleagues along the way before easing his way into the crowded space, where the speakers had already begun.

Truthfully, he was proud as hell of his adopted brother, Jackson, for taking on the incident commander position for this latest hurricane. His brother was the hardest-working EMT in the area, and the promotion and recognition that came with it had been a long time coming for Jackson. He hoped everything went to plan and his brother got the new job he wanted. No one deserved it more than Jackson, but then, life didn't always give us what we deserved.

Silently, he moved in beside his brother now and leaned back against the wall, grateful for the dimmed lights in the room as he stared up at the podium and the presenter.

Stacy Williams.

The name suited her—steady, sure, sensible, sexy as hell yet completely unassuming.

It was that last one that had his throat constricting with adrenaline as long-ago memories assailed him. Still hushed, still shadowed. But then they'd been on the beach, just the two of them beneath the moonlight, huddled on a blanket, entwined in each other's arms, the stars the only witness as they'd made love on the sand dune and his world had been rocked forever.

That had been the night before he'd left to go to Myanmar. The night when the future had seemed so uncertain and the only tangible thing he'd had to hold on to had been her. If he closed his eyes, he could still remember the feel of her silky skin against him, hear her soft cries as she came undone in his arms, taste the sweetness of her kisses on his lips...

"Everything okay?" Jackson asked, giving him some serious side-eye.

"Fine," Luis said, shaking off the unwanted warmth inside him. It had been one night, a drunken fling. It didn't mean anything at all. Even if it kind of felt like it did, at least to him. He wasn't really a one-night-stand kind of man. Wasn't a relationship guy at all, honestly. He didn't have the time.

Too busy taking care of others. Always putting others' wants and needs ahead of his own.

He was a doctor. That's what he did. Who he was.

"And now I'll turn things back over to IC Jackson Durand," Stacy said before heading back to her seat, her gaze briefly meeting Luis's before flickering away again.

Luis's gut clenched. She recognized him. She *knew*.

They'd never spoken after that night. He'd left the US early the next morning on his flight, and she'd gone back to Miami, he'd assumed. They'd both gotten on with their lives, obviously. But in that brief meeting of their eyes, he'd seen her blue ones widen slightly and Luis knew she'd been remembering that night, too. Before he caught himself, he was moving across the room to stand closer to where she was sitting. He had no intention of rekindling old flames, but he did want to talk to her, to dispel the awkward tension between them, especially since he'd seen her earlier with the injured firefighter and chances were they might run into each other again.

After all, they were both on the ERT team and Luis was coordinating the ER to handle any casualties the storm might cause. A good working relationship with the fire department was key to any response plan. He was just doing his job.

And perhaps, if he told himself that enough times, he might actually believe it.

First, though, Luis needed to get through this damned meeting.

Which seemed to drag on and on and on.

He got up and gave his presentation about the hospital's contingency plans and triage protocols during disasters. With Key West and the surrounding islands in the hot zone for hurricanes, it wasn't uncommon for them to experience several each season. This year had been worse, though, with more named storms than any on record so far, and it didn't appear that it would let up anytime soon.

When he was done, Luis made his way back over to where Stacy sat with another woman, Lucy Miller. Luis recognized her and her therapy dog from the days they made their rounds upstairs in the children's ward. He had to admit he was a bit shocked to see Lucy here, given her anxiety disorders, but then, he of all people should know that being neurodivergent didn't preclude one from doing whatever one put one's mind to. In fact, for him at least, his mild case of Asperger's syndrome actually benefited his work as a doctor, made him more focused, better able to retain and use information about his patients. And yes, sometimes the social aspects were still a struggle for him, even after years of adapting, but people loved to talk about themselves, so as long as he kept that spotlight pointed away from himself and firmly on them, he was fine.

"All right, folks," Jackson said from the podium. "That's it for today. Please keep one eye on the weather reports, and if predictions change, I'll let everyone know and we'll meet again. Thank you."

People began to file out of the room, and Stacy whispered something to Lucy before standing, pushing her chair in then heading for the door. It was now or never, and Luis's pulse kicked up a notch.

He was hardly some fumbling schoolboy, unsure and untested around women, but for some reason the thought of talking to this woman made him nervous as hell. Maybe because he'd relived that night five years ago in his head so many times during the lonely days in between that he'd built it into something completely magical and fantastic. Maybe reality would never equal the dream. Maybe this was all a horrible mistake.

Before he could stop himself, Luis touched her arm just as she reached the door and she turned, the end of her long blond ponytail brushing the back of his hand and sending a slight shiver through him. Her blue eyes widened, just as pretty and deep azure as he remembered, and just like that, Luis felt like he was drowning. He choked out words past his tight vocal cords. "It is you."

CHAPTER TWO

HER FIRST IMPULSE was to feign ignorance, but from the way he'd been watching her this whole time, it was clear he'd recognized her, so what was the point? Besides, the last thing Stacy wanted to do was draw more attention to her past indiscretions, so she hiked her chin toward the other members of her fire crew to go on out into the hall, then waited until they were gone before turning back to face Luis.

"It is." She forced a smile she didn't feel and looked him over. Man, he was still gorgeous as ever. At first, when she'd looked back on that night, she'd figured she'd been imagining that thick, curly dark hair, those velvety caramel-colored eyes, the impossibly long eyelashes that most women would kill for. Of course, then, as luck would have it, her own son was born with those same features nine months later, so…

Stacy swallowed hard and did her best to cover her nervousness with chatter. "Didn't think I'd see you again. How are you? You look well."

Luis blinked at her a moment, a slight frown lining the smooth skin between his dark brows. "I wondered what happened to you after that night, if you were okay."

That slight accent of his sent a sudden shiver of unwanted awareness through her, taking her right back to that night on the beach, the stars twinkling above, his strong arms around her, sweet endearments on his lips as he'd moved over her, in her, so careful, so tender, so...

"I'm fine. Great, actually." She needed air, and space. The walls of the room seemed to be closing in on her with him that close, his warmth and scent surrounding her—soap and sandalwood. Stacy turned fast and pushed out into the hallway, grateful for the bright lights and noise of the other meeting members to distract her. She pointed at her badge and headed down the corridor toward the entrance to the ER. "Captain now."

"I see that," Luis said, keeping pace beside her, adjusting his long-legged stride to accommodate her shorter one. Funny how that worked. She was a good six inches shorter than him, but that night they'd fit perfectly together.

Stop thinking about that night. Stop it.

"Are you living in Key West now?" he asked as they passed her fire crew, who were giving her curious looks.

"I am," she said, leaving it at that. She and Miguel had moved into a nice apartment at a local complex the previous year when she'd taken the captain's job here after leaving her department in Miami. "And you? Are you still traveling the world on your mission trips?"

"No. Not anymore," he said, tapping the square metal handicapped button on the wall with his elbow so the automatic doors swung open ahead of them. "I've taken the position as head of the emergency department here at Key West General, so I'm staying put now."

"Good to know." Actually, it wasn't good. Not at all. Because if they were both staying here in Key West, that meant she needed to tell him about Miguel. Honestly, Stacy had never meant to keep it a secret from Luis for this long. It was just that once she'd found out she was pregnant, he was long gone, and she'd had no way to get a hold of him. Then she'd had the baby and had to fend for herself, and she'd been too busy working and surviving to consider another trip back down to Key West to search for Luis. Being accepted into the fire academy training program had been a godsend—good pay, good benefits, good exercise and a new, extended family she'd always wanted but never dreamed she'd have. The guys in the Miami-Dade County Fire and Rescue Department had embraced Stacy and Miguel as their own, giving her son all the attention and positive male role models he could ever want or need.

Still, having a father—*his* father—in his life was important for her son, at least to Stacy. So, no matter how awkward, she would tell Luis. Just maybe when the time and place were more appropriate.

"You work with Reed?" Luis asked as they stopped near the nurses' station in the bustling ER. "The injured firefighter?"

"I do. He's on a different crew than mine, but we're all in the same battalion." She swallowed hard against the lingering constriction in her throat. "It's like a big family."

"That's nice," Luis said, turning his attention to a chart the nurse behind the desk handed him. "Your colleague is in for a tough battle."

"Is there any word on how the surgery

went?" she asked, glad for a topic of discussion.

"I can't discuss the specifics because of privacy laws, but suffice it to say that when I left the OR upstairs, he was holding his own. With luck they got the bleeding under control and we can move on to evaluating his leg injury."

"Will he walk again?"

"I can't give you a prognosis on that at the moment, I'm afraid." Luis continued jotting notes in the chart he was working on. "It will be a long recovery either way. Given the extent of the initial injury, there will be nerve and tissue damage that will take time to heal. Physical therapy and bed rest are definitely in his future whether he keeps that leg or not. It will just depend on what the focus is— restoring strength and mobility or retraining him to use a prosthetic."

"Will he be able to return to active duty as a firefighter?" Stacy asked, her heart aching for his family and what they were going through. "He'll have his pension, but I know Reed, and he'd hate sitting behind a desk all day."

"We won't know until after the surgery and the ortho consult." He glanced over at her. "But if everything works out well,

I don't see why not. They've made huge strides in technology and many people with prosthetics can do just as well, and in some cases better, than their counterparts without disabilities. That would be up to your department, however, and what the physical therapists have to say once they work with and evaluate him. We're getting way ahead of ourselves here, though."

Now that Stacy had a chance to really study him as he worked, she could see tiny lines near the corners of his eyes that hadn't been there before, and a hint of dark stubble just beneath the surface of his strong jaw. She wondered how long his shift had been, if he had someone waiting at home for him once he was done...

Not that it was any of her business. Nope. She was not looking for a relationship. She had plenty enough on her plate as it was with work and Miguel and now the hurricane heading in their general direction. It was just that if he was involved with someone else, that would add another dimension to him finding out he had a son from a previous liaison. She needed to tread carefully, since the last thing Miguel needed right now was more upset to his schedule. With his mild Asperger's, routine was the glue that held their little world together. And most of all, she didn't want her son hurt.

As someone who knew the pain of being an only child, raised by a single mother, Stacy knew all too well the pain of letting someone in, only to have them walk away or disappoint you. She remembered when her own father had walked out on them. At first, she'd cried and cried, running to the window each time a car drove by their house, thinking it might be him. Then, after a while, she'd turned the pain and hurt inward, thinking it was her fault he was gone. That it must've been something she'd done, or if she'd only been better, somehow, her father wouldn't have left them. Eventually she'd internalized that feeling of never being enough and translated it into constantly pushing herself to do more, be more, hoping someday it might be enough to keep those she loved from leaving.

Stacy refused to have her son experience that same trauma by exposing Miguel to a man who might just as likely disappear from their lives as quickly as he'd arrived. She'd never really explained to Miguel about where his father was, and luckily he hadn't asked. It had always just been the two of them. Now, though, as he was getting older, she feared the questions would come and, with them, the knowledge that he'd been a surprise baby. But in the best possible way. Stacy couldn't image her life without her son. He was her reason for being, her reason for getting up every day, her reason for everything.

There wasn't anything she wouldn't do for Miguel, including telling Luis the truth.

Soon. Just not yet.

They stood there a moment, neither knowing what to say, until finally Stacy spotted Reed's wife and daughter in the hall and seized on her opportunity to escape. "Uh, I should get back to my crew and Reed's family. Excuse me. It was nice seeing you again."

"I'd like to have dinner," Luis said as she was walking away, halting her in her tracks. "To discuss coordination of our protocols for the hurricane."

Her heart thudded harder against her rib cage. The hurricane. Right. "Uh, I…"

"Stacy," he said, handing the chart back to the nurse then stepping toward her, a hint of his tanned chest visible through the vee of his light green scrub shirt. She concentrated there and not on his eyes, those too-perceptive eyes that sent tingles of heat through her like fireworks and always saw way more than she wanted to reveal. Like how nervous she was around him. Like how he still

affected her, even after all these years. Like
how almost five years later and a lifetime of
changes apart, her attraction to him burned
bright as the sun. "Just dinner. That's all.
How about tonight? Say, 8:00 p.m., after my
shift? Unless you have other plans already."

There it was. Her out. She seized on it with
both hands, even as she cursed herself a cow-
ard. "Actually, I do have other plans tonight.
Sorry." Namely, mac and cheese and home-
work with Miguel. "Maybe another time."

She took off before he could ask any more
questions, the weight of his stare prickling
the back of her neck all the way down the
corridor.

Luis went back to work, seeing patients and
finishing his shift in the ER before going
upstairs to check on Reed's progress before
going home for the night. The man's family had moved upstairs to the private waiting area near the ICU. Luis peeked in as he
passed by and spotted the orthopedic surgeon in with them, giving them a post-op
update. Stacy was there, too, glancing up to
meet Luis's gaze before quickly refocusing
her attention back on the doctor.

He didn't want to intrude, but from where

he stood, Luis could overhear part of what his colleague was saying to them.

"So the good news is, we were able to re-establish blood flow to his leg, okay," the orthopedic surgeon said. "The bad news is, his leg was without blood flow for a significant period of time."

A quiet murmur passed through the family before the wife asked, "What are your biggest concerns then, for tonight?"

"Well, I won't lie," the surgeon said, sighing. "There are a lot of hurdles to get over before we can save his leg."

It was as Luis had thought. He turned away then to go back downstairs, this time using the elevators, because damn, he was tired. He pushed the button and waited, staring up at the digital numbers above the shiny metal doors. Having a conversation like that with the family was tough. One of the toughest parts of the job, frankly, regardless of what area of medicine you practiced. Human nature made you want to offer as much hope as possible to them, but conscience and scientific fact meant you also needed to be very realistic about the possible outcomes and set realistic expectations for everyone involved. It was a tightrope he walked daily in the ER, especially with the more severe trauma cases such as Reed's.

In truth, those conversations were the ones that kept him up at night, worrying about the patient's future. And even though Luis wasn't in charge of the man's case any longer, releasing that responsibility was not so easy to do. Regardless of his exhaustion, Luis was pretty certain he'd lose plenty of sleep worrying about whether Reed would be able to return to his career as a firefighter.

It was just part of who he was, to worry, to overanalyze, to think things to death.

Like his conversation with Stacy earlier.

That night five years ago, he'd had no idea that she'd wanted to be a firefighter. Not that they'd discussed their future plans or talked about anything at all much beyond that moment, but she'd not struck him as an adrenaline junkie or a risk taker. In fact, back then she'd seemed the epitome of the South Florida party girl, a wild, reckless, devil-may-care woman on spring break looking to have a good time and leave her cares and concerns behind. She'd told him she was twenty-two that night, but there'd been a maturity in her eyes and in her heart that went well beyond her age. Of course, once he'd looked into those wide blue eyes of hers he'd been lost anyway, and fighting his attraction to her had gone right out the window. Jackson and some of his buddies from his residency program had taken Luis out as a farewell party before his flight to Bangkok the next morning to begin his mission trip. And what a send-off it was. They'd taken over his parents' pub and partied until well after midnight. Needing a break from the noise and revelry, Luis had excused himself to take a walk on the beach and he'd found Stacy outside as well, staring up at the starry sky.

Their chemistry had been instant, as had the fiery passion between them.

She'd taken his hand as they'd strolled across the moonlit sand. Then, once they'd left the thumping music and raucous cheers of the pub behind, he'd kissed her. Neither of them was completely sober, but they both had surrendered willingly to the desire shimmering between them. Being with her had been both a revelation and a curse. Stacy had been like no one else he'd ever been with before—so soft and sweet and exquisitely responsive to his every touch and kiss and nuzzle. But that same uniqueness had also been a curse, because he'd never forgotten her, or that night. Not in nearly five long years. And now, seeing her again so unexpectedly today had shaken him to his core, and…

"Seems we can't avoid each other today."
Ding!

Stacy stood a few feet away, looking anywhere but at him. "I can, uh…" She pointed toward the stairwell door across the corridor. "I'll just take the steps."

"Don't be silly," Luis said, tired of playing the avoidance game. He held the elevators doors open for her. "We're both adults. I think we can handle this."

She stood there a moment, her expression uncertain, then seemed to reach a decision and boarded the elevator beside him with a decisive nod. "True."

Luis pushed the buttons for the first floor then stepped back and clasped his hands in front of him as the doors swished closed. He stared down at his toes while Stacy stared straight ahead, his stomach lurching as the car jolted then began to descend.

"So," he said after a moment, unable to tolerate the choking silence any longer. "Reed came through his surgery okay."

"Yes," Stacy said. "The prognosis for his leg is still uncertain, though. Just like you mentioned earlier."

"Yes." The elevator stopped on the second

floor and a little old lady who looked like someone's grandmother got on. She smiled and nodded to Luis then Stacy, then turned and faced the doors, her large tote bag with knitting needles sticking out the top nearly poking him in the leg. Luis stepped back and cleared his throat. "My thoughts are with his family during this difficult time."

"Mine, too." Stacy took a deep breath. "Look, Luis. I'm sorry about earlier, if I seemed abrupt. I was just surprised to see you and I've been busy and have a lot on my plate at the moment and—"

Ding!

The doors opened on the first floor and Luis sidled around the woman and her knitting needles to stick his arms against the door to hold it so Stacy could get out then followed her into the corridor. He waited until the elevator closed again before taking Stacy's arm and leading her down the hall to a quieter area for privacy.

"No need to apologize. I think we were both thrown before. But my offer still stands." He checked his watch then put his hands on his hips and looked at her. "My shift is done. I'm heading home. We can still grab dinner if you'd like."

"Oh, I can't tonight. Sorry." She pulled

out her phone. "I've got things at the apartment to handle."

"Okay. Fair enough. How about tomorrow night, then?" He pulled up his schedule on his smart watch. "I'm off the whole day, but I have plans until later in the afternoon. How about dinner after that? Say, seven at the pub?"

"Durand's Duck Bill Pub?" She glanced up at him, her expression surprised. "I haven't been there in years."

"All the more reason to go, then." He smiled. He'd been planning to help out his adopted parents tomorrow anyway, doing odd jobs for them around the bar, same as he'd done since joining their family at the age of six. "I doubt the place has changed that much since the last time you saw it. More flags, probably. And T-shirts."

"Oh, I remember those." She grinned, and his night suddenly brightened. Her smile faltered, though, as her phone buzzed with a new message. Stacy frowned at the screen, then swallowed hard, putting the device back in her pocket then taking a deep breath, as if her decision was a difficult one. "Okay. Fine. Yes. Dinner tomorrow night sounds good. We have a lot to talk about."

Luis nodded, adding the event to his calendar. He wasn't sure what exactly they needed to discuss, but he was glad for the chance to get reacquainted with her and see if his memories did her justice or if he'd somehow turned her into some kind of fantasy in his mind. "Great. Tomorrow night at seven, then. I'll probably be behind the bar when you get there, in case you can't find me."

She gave him a quizzical look. "You work there, too?"

"No." He chuckled. "Well, not on the official payroll, anyway. But you help out family when you can."

"Oh, right. I forgot." A brief shadow flickered across her pretty face, so fast he would've missed it if he hadn't been watching her so closely. "Well, then. I guess I'll see you there."

"You will." He stood in the hall as she backed away from him, neither of them looking away until finally the automatic doors of the ER swished open behind her and she disappeared into the darkness outside. Luis sighed and shook his head, then turned on his heel to head to the staff locker room to change, an odd mix of apprehension and anticipation simmering inside him. He shouldn't get excited about their dinner tomorrow. It was nothing more than two strangers meeting for a meal.

Two strangers who'd had sex. On the beach. Beneath the stars and moon, her skin glowing and her eyes bright with passion. If he closed his eyes, Luis swore he could still hear his name on her lips as she climaxed around him, could still feel the heat of her tight against his skin, could still taste her sweetness on his tongue.

God, he was getting sentimental and silly with fatigue.

That had to be it. Fantasy indeed.

He was a man who lived by logic. He prized truth and facts and science above all else. He didn't deal with emotions and intuition, because those things only ever got you in trouble. Those things could cost you everything, if you weren't careful. Take his birth parents. They'd ignored the obvious danger of crossing the strong currents and shark-infested waters of the Straits of Florida at night, plus the weather reports at that time heralding the impending arrival of a tropical storm, in order to give young Luis and themselves a chance at a better life. That effort had cost them their lives and left Luis an orphan. Luckily, the Durands had taken him in shortly after he'd entered foster care, and they'd given him a good life, the life his birth parents would've wanted for him. But still...

No. Luis was a man with a purpose. One he took seriously, without his emotions getting in the way.

Except for that one night almost five years ago with Stacy. That had been all about his feelings...

He changed into his street clothes and headed home to his secluded, lush beachfront property on the north side of the island of Key West, unable to shake the odd sense of inevitability that there was more happening between him and Stacy than just the past. Luis pulled into his driveway and cut the engine on his Mercedes then sat there staring at the white facade of his modern two-story luxury home. He'd worked hard for his good life and enjoyed the perks it bought him, but he also gave generously of both his time and money to local charities to help the underprivileged and refugees, having been both himself once upon a time.

Yep. There was definitely a reason fate had brought the two of them together again. And tomorrow night, Luis intended to find out exactly what that reason was.

CHAPTER THREE

STACY HEARD THE music pouring out of the open doors of the bar on the corner of Duval and Greene Streets before she ever reached the entrance of the Duck Bill Pub. A blend of calypso and pop, the song had a catchy beat and an island vibe that had her toes tapping in her strappy sandals.

With each step she took, it felt like the past five years slipped away a bit more. She'd not been back here since moving to Key West the prior year because there were just too many memories, too much water under the proverbial bridge, but now…

Well, now she had important business to take care of. Namely telling Luis about the son he didn't know he had. She owed that to him, and she owed it to Miguel.

If only she could get the nervous butterflies in her stomach to settle down, she'd be all set.

A small crowd had already gathered near the entrance, waiting to get in. Duval Street was famous with the tourists anyway, and Durand's Duck Bill Pub was practically a legend in these parts. It was why she and her friends had come that first night, to see the place where Hemingway used to hang out with his buddies and maybe pick up a T-shirt and a hangover as souvenirs.

What she'd ended up with after spending the night on the beach with Luis, however, had changed her life forever.

As she crossed the street at the light and approached the bouncer outside, the band ended their song to thunderous applause. She stopped near the door and leaned closer to the bulky guard to say, "I'm supposed to be meeting Luis Durand at the bar?"

The guy nodded and pointed. "Go on in. He's waiting for you."

"Thanks." She wove through the people milling about and the tables packed with patrons toward the large curved bar in the back corner of the place. It didn't look much different in there than the last time—shiny tile floors, paneled walls covered with local memorabilia and photos of the owners with visiting celebrities, and those flags hanging from the exposed beams in the ceiling. Each time a visitor from a new country arrived at the Duck Bill, they hung the person's native flag from the rafters. According to the tally sign on the wall, the pub was up to 178. Impressive, given there were only 195 total in the world. Seemed it really was the Crossroads of the Keys, as the pub's slogan proclaimed.

And speaking of crossroads…

Stacy finally reached the bar and squeezed between two sets of patrons to ask the bartender about Luis, except when she opened her mouth, no words came out, because the bartender *was* Luis.

He glanced up at her then went back to mixing the cocktail he was working on before doing a double take and grinning. "Hello."

"Hello." She watched him assemble two complicated-looking beverages with a mix of alcohols and fizzy water and fruit then deliver them to a server waiting farther down the bar before returning to her. He looked different tonight, out of his scrubs and wearing one the Duck Bill Pub's logo T-shirts like the rest of the staff. Honestly, he looked younger in his casual jeans. Younger and most definitely sexier.

She swallowed hard against the sudden, unwanted lump of awareness in her throat.

"Working a side hustle?" she asked as he slung a dish towel over one muscled shoulder, those warm caramel-colored eyes of his watching her far too closely for her comfort. Humor and snark were always her fallbacks when she was nervous, and she hoped they'd help her out of her awkwardness now. "Maybe they need to pay you more at the hospital."

"They pay me just fine," he said, leaning one hand on the bar, his teeth even and white against his tanned skin. "Can I get you something to drink?"

"Oh, uh…" She hadn't even bothered to look at the menu, hadn't noticed anything but him since she'd arrived at the bar. Stacy shook her head and glanced over at what the other bartender was making. Something tall and frothy and bright pink with what looked like a flamingo head sticking out of it. "I'll take one of those, if it's not too much trouble."

"No trouble at all," he said, his gaze narrowing for a fraction of a second, as if he was trying to figure out something about her and then did, before he cocked his head. "One Hot Pink Barbie coming up."

While he made her drink, she studied him more closely. He was muscled but not bulky, more sinewy and lithe, moving with a grace that most dancers would envy. That was one thing she remembered about Luis from that night. Well…one of the things. Every move he made seemed purposeful, like he wanted to get everything done as efficiently as possible. She saw the same grace in Miguel.

Her son, too, shared his father's dark curly hair and easy smile. Sometimes, at night, when she closed her eyes, she swore she could still feel the silky strands between her fingers, feel the scrape of his stubbled jaw on her neck as he nuzzled her throat, feel the warm strength of his arms around her as he'd called out her name as he climaxed inside her beneath the stars. The moment they'd made Miguel. The moment her future had swerved onto an entirely new and unexpected path…

The moment that connected them even now.

Tell him.

Luis returned with her drink, and she took a sip for courage. Fruity with a hint of rum and mint for balance. Delicious. She tucked her hair behind her ear then glanced around the busy place. "Any chance we can find a quiet spot to talk in here?"

"Of course." He came around from behind the bar and placed his hand at the small of her back, deftly guiding her through the crowd to a smaller room near the back of the place. There were fewer people in here, and Luis led her to a table for two in the corner with a Reserved sign on it. "I set it aside for us earlier."

"Great."

They took their seats and he removed the towel from his shoulder, twisting it in his hands atop the table. It hadn't occurred to her that he might be nervous, too, but based on his body language, they were both on pins and needles here.

"So," she said, fiddling with the flamingo straw in her glass to distract herself from the enormity of what she had to tell him. "Uh, your parents are doing well?"

"Yes, fine." He smiled, still staring down at his hands. "They are up in Miami right now, and I told them to stay up there until after the storm passes, just to be on the safe side. The staff here can handle things until they get back."

"Is that why you were bartending tonight?"

"What?" He frowned slightly then shook his head. "No. We had someone call in sick at the last minute and I was here waiting for you, so I filled in until the replacement arrived, that's all."

"Ah." She sipped a little more of her drink, careful not to have too much alcohol on her empty stomach. She knew all too well where that could lead. "Right. Well, um." *Just tell him already.* "There's something I, uh, wanted to talk to you about tonight…"

"Are you hungry?" Luis asked, glancing up at her. "We have a full menu now. Sandwiches, steaks, seafood, salads, whatever you like. My treat."

"Oh." She blinked at him a moment. "Uh, okay. I didn't eat lunch today, so I'm starved."

"Excellent." He stood and grinned down at her again, the smile that made her toes curl in her sandals. "Allow me to choose for you? Do you have any allergies? Any foods you dislike?"

"No allergies," she said. "And nothing too spicy, please."

"Got it." He held up a finger then walked over to talk to the man behind a second, smaller bar. The guy nodded as Luis spoke then turned to type an order into the computer behind him while Luis returned to their table. "Done. Our appetizers should be out soon. Now, please. Tell me what you wanted to discuss. We know so little about each other, really."

True enough.

She'd been thinking that same thing earlier on her way here. Weird how you could share such intimacy with a person and yet not know their middle name, or their birthday, or even their favorite color or food. Then again, that was kind of the point of one-night stands. No ties, no strings, no messy details to clean up later.

Oh God.

In her mind, Stacy had imagined a million times how this moment would go, how she'd tell Miguel's father about him, but this was nothing like what she'd pictured in her head. Where they sat in the shadowed corner gave them a modicum of privacy, but you could still hear the raucous cheers from the crowd in the main bar, the twang and percussion of the steel drum band, smell the scent of the fried food and the hint of booze in the air.

So very much like the night they'd met five years ago, and yet so different.

Growing up the only child of a single mom in a poor neighborhood in Miami, Stacy had learned early on how to take care of herself and how to handle difficult situations—

head-on, direct, deal with it and be done. It was one of the things that made her so good at her job as a firefighter. But now, those skills failed her. She had no clue how to broach the subject with him in a way that wouldn't smack of secrets and lies.

No. Not lies. She'd never lied to him about Miguel. She'd just omitted telling Luis about him. And it wasn't for lack of wanting to. He'd been out of the country. Unreachable. She'd had to get on with things for her own survival. And then time had passed, and life moved on. Now that they were both here, she was doing the responsible thing and letting him know. How he chose to deal with the news was his business. She didn't expect anything from him, hadn't even mentioned anything to Miguel, in case things didn't go well tonight. The last thing she wanted was for her son to be hurt by any of this.

Miguel had never asked about his father up until now, but at four, that was bound to change soon.

Right.

She took a deep breath and exhaled slowly, nervous heat prickling her cheeks. "Do you remember our night together years ago?"

Luis met her gaze then, warmth and wariness burning in them. "Yes." The word emerged gruffly. "One does not forget so easily."

Her chest squeezed. That was accurate enough. She'd lost count of how many times she'd relived that night on the beach, the pleasure she'd found in his arms, the hollow ache that persisted inside her. She'd never been a fling sort of girl, her only one being with him, and Luis had left an impression on her, in more ways than one.

"No." Her mouth dried and her mind whirled, but she forced herself to keep going. "Um, there's something you need to know about that night. Something that happened…"

"Oh God," he said, sitting back on his seat to rake a hand through his hair, rocking back on the rear legs of his chair. "I didn't hurt you, did I? I was pretty far gone that night, and parts are a bit murky."

"No, no. You didn't hurt me," she said. *Not in the way you think.* "It's more…um…" *God, just say it.* "I got pregnant. That night. We didn't use anything, and…"

His eyes widened slightly, and his mouth opened, closed, then opened again. The chair plunked down flatly. "I'm sorry. I don't—what?"

"I got pregnant that night, Luis. I had a baby. A son. Our son. Miguel."

Time seemed to slow around Luis, and the room tunneled as he took that in. A million words raced through his head at once, but all he managed to say was "I have a son?"

"Yes."

She sat back as the server brought a large platter filled with all sorts of beer-battered, deep-fried goodies. Too bad Luis's appetite had vanished.

"His name is Miguel, after my father. He's four," she said once they were alone again, fiddling with her napkin, her fingers trembling slightly. "He's smart and sensitive and quiet. He was diagnosed with a mild case of Asperger's syndrome, which is on the—"

"Autism scale. I know." Luis couldn't quite get his brain working properly. He scrubbed a hand over his face, hoping to wipe away some of the shock. A son. A family he knew nothing about. There were so many questions in his mind.

Before he could ask any of them, though, Stacy held up a hand to stop him. "I'm not telling you any of this because I want anything from you. I just felt you should know.

Miguel and I have done fine on our own, and nothing will change that."

That brought Luis up short, finally jarring him from his daze. "Wait. Are you saying you don't want me to meet him?"

"No. He's your son and I don't intend to deny you your parental rights, but I want you to think long and hard about it before you decide. He's a very special boy and he means the world to me. I don't want to see him hurt. So, if you don't intend to stick around and become a meaningful part of his life going forward, it might be best for you to not start anything with him at all."

He opened his mouth, then closed it. He could hardly believe this was really happening, but it was. He'd always wanted children of his own someday, once he got settled, got his life in order, got past the lingering fears from his childhood that he might not be around to take care of his own family.

Oh God.

His son had been living without him for the last four years and done just fine, apparently. So much time lost, so many things he'd missed. So few chances to get any of it back or get it right now. He sat there, watching Stacy from across the table, his gut twisted in knots. There was no doubt in his mind she was telling him the truth. The fact his son had inherited his Asperger's just clinched it.

Welcome to fatherhood.

"I, uh… Wow," he said at last, shaking his head, sitting forward to clasp his hands atop the table. "I have no idea what I'm doing here. And you're right. I don't want to see the boy hurt, either. If I'm not planning on maintaining a relationship with him, then I should steer clear. But what if I do want to be a part of his life?"

Stacy halted midbite as she nibbled on a piece of calamari and stared at him, eyes wide. "Oh, well…" She swallowed hard and set the food back on her plate, wiping her fingers on her napkin. "Then I guess we should talk about that, then." She exhaled slowly then sat forward, too, looking as discombobulated as he felt. "Sorry. I honestly wasn't sure what to expect when I came here tonight. It's a lot. I know. Trust me, I know. And I want you to know that I would have told you sooner, but when I tried to contact you after I first found out, they told me you were gone and they weren't sure when you were coming back to the States and I needed to find a job to support myself and figure out what to do about the baby and…"

He frowned. "No, no. I understand. I do."

Luis raked a hand through his hair. "I don't blame you. I just…did you not think to try to find me sooner? I mean yes, you tried when you were first pregnant, but what about after that?" He cursed and shook his head. "Sorry. That didn't come out right. We were both responsible for what happened that night on the beach. I shouldn't put it all on you. I could have checked on you, too, once I was back in the States."

"True." She looked up at him. "I guess we both should have tried harder."

Luis gave a curt nod then watched her as she picked up her calamari again. "Did you go back to Miami?"

"I did. Lived with my mother for a while as I went through the fire academy, then once I graduated and was hired onto the force, I got my own place for myself and Miguel. It wasn't anything fancy, but it did all right for us."

"That must've been hard, working fulltime with a baby at home." His chest constricted with guilt and worry. If only he'd known, he'd have helped her, supported her. Then again, he'd been busy himself, establishing his practice at the hospital and working his way up in the department. Who's to say that he would've reacted honorably? He liked to think he would, but given his own issues and anxieties, he might also have handled things badly.

Or worse than he already was.

"It was tough, not going to lie. More so after my mom got sick with breast cancer." She finished her food then pushed her plate away, not looking at him, her voice cracking. "She used to watch Miguel for me sometimes, but then she got so sick from the chemo. Thankfully she beat it in the end, and we all moved back to Key West after to start over again."

"Oh God. I'm so sorry, Stacy." And now he felt like an even bigger ass, if that were possible. "If I'd known this was going on, I would have been there for you, for both of you." He reached over and took her hand without thinking. "I'm really sorry."

"It's okay. You didn't know." She shrugged, pulled away. "And I don't need your pity. He doesn't know about you," she said, her cheeks pinkening. "Miguel. He's never really asked about his father, and I haven't told him anything. So, if you want out, tell me. We can both continue on as we have been."

Regret dug sharp claws into his belly. He'd only been two years older than his son was now when he'd lost his parents, and Luis would give anything to have them back, to have just one more day with them. Now that he knew about Miguel, no way could he abandon him. And yes, his schedule was busy, impossibly so. But he'd find a way to be there for his son, if that's what he chose to do, because it was important.

"What if I want in?" he asked. "What if I want to be a part of his life going forward?"

"Then we need to—" Before she could finish her sentence, her phone buzzed in her purse and she pulled it out. "I'm sorry. It's the department. I really need to take this. Excuse me for a second."

Luis sat back as she got up and wandered out a nearby door to the patio outside.

He had a son. A son named Miguel who he'd had no idea existed. If the ground beneath his feet had opened and swallowed him whole, Luis couldn't have been more stunned than he was right then. But he needed to pull it together and find a way through this. He was someone whom everyone else depended on, the person who got things done. Continuing on as they had been wouldn't work for him, not anymore. Not with his child's future on the line.

Many times over the years he'd wondered what must've driven his parents to take that fateful journey across the treacherous straits in the middle of the night in a rickety boat, to risk everything on an uncertain outcome.

Now, as he sat there staring through the glass at Stacy pacing back and forth on the patio as she talked on her phone, he finally knew the answer.

Some things were worth the risk.

Miguel was worth the risk to him. Even if it cost him everything.

And as Stacy looked up and caught his eye, he realized it just might.

CHAPTER FOUR

THE NEXT TWO days were crazy busy, and Stacy was glad because they kept her mind off Luis and focused on her work. She gripped the edge of her seat in the back of the fire truck as they rounded a corner, lights and sirens blazing.

They were on their way to an accident scene, having received a report of a car in a ditch with victims trapped inside. Fire rescue would need to use the Jaws of Life to cut them out. As they sped toward the disaster, Stacy couldn't help wishing there was an equivalent tool she could use to get her out of the mess she'd made of things last night.

She couldn't seem to get the expression on his face when she'd told him about Miguel out of her head. Stunned, then scared, then stoic. And while he'd said he wanted to be involved in their son's life, well, didn't all fathers say that? Her own dad certainly had, then he'd just left one day and never come back. Stacy had waited all night on the porch for him, refusing to leave, until finally she'd had to admit to herself that she'd never see him again.

No way in hell Stacy would ever put Miguel through that. She'd rather him never know his father then grow up hurting because Luis changed his mind at some point.

"We're here!" Rob, the firefighter driving the truck, shouted to the crew in the back. He eased the large vehicle in between several parked squad cars and an ambulance. "Pretty overgrown. Looks like it's going to be tough getting them out."

Stacy and the rest of her crew climbed out of the back and came face-to-face with a thick wall of foliage. At first she saw nothing but trees and bushes, with the occasional fallen log that could've been mistaken for something else. But then one of the police officers on scene pointed to a barely visible curve of black jutting out from the bottom of the steep embankment.

"There's definitely someone trapped in the car," the officer said above the roar of the fire truck's engine, the reflection in his sunglasses alternating red and blue from the lights. "Condensation on the inside of the windows from their breath. Looks like whoever was driving hit a tree there." He pointed to a massive oak a few feet away with a large gouge where the bark had been sheared off. "The impact crumpled the front of the vehicle. Airbags deployed."

"Right." Stacy made her way carefully down the embankment, her boots slipping on the loose soil, until she reached the vehicle along with two other members of the crew. Phil made his way around to the passenger side of the vehicle while she took the driver's side, heart racing and blood pounding in her ears. She yanked on the handle of the dented door on her side, but it didn't budge. Phil tried his side, too, with no luck, either. The ground down here was muddier and slippery, and they both struggled to stay upright as they tried each of the rear doors as well with no luck. "John, go get the cutters."

"Will do, boss," the younger guy said, trekking back up the hill to return a few minutes later with the hydraulic blades they called the Jaws of Life. He and another firefighter made short work of the driver's side door, careful not to further injure the victim inside, then stepped back so Stacy could assess her patient.

As she stepped near the wrecked vehicle

again, a pained groan issued from the person inside, and her chest constricted. The noise was actually a good sign. Noise meant the victim was still alive. Stacy leaned inside the car to check the pulse of the woman behind the wheel. Maybe midtwenties, dressed in shorts and flip-flops, the hint of a bikini top beneath her T-shirt and the distinct smell of alcohol on her breath. Unfortunately, drunk driving was an all-too-common occurrence down in the Keys. As she counted the woman's heart rate, she checked her respirations as well. Both normal. That was good, at least.

"Ma'am?" she said, patting the groggy woman's cheek. "My name is Stacy Williams. I'm with the Key West Fire Department. We're going to get you out of here, okay?"

The woman squinted open one eye at her words, then her dark eyes widened like saucers with instant panic. "What happened?"

"Looks like you went off the road, hit a tree," Stacy said, seeing the woman's slight nod. "You're very lucky to be alive," she said looking at Phil over the roof of the car.

After palpating the woman's arms, shoulders and chest for injuries, she checked her pupils, then glanced down toward her legs.

Not good. The collision had caused the dashboard to collapse, pinning both of the victim's legs in place.

Phil ducked his head in through the passenger side while Stacy bent to retrieve the woman's purse from where it was wedged in the foot well and riffled through it to find ID. The woman's name was Alicia. Meanwhile, the EMTs made their way down the embankment as well to check the victim's blood pressure, made more difficult by the fact they couldn't move her out of her seat.

"Alicia, stay with us, okay?" Stacy said.

The woman grunted and opened her eyes again.

"Can you tell me where you're hurting?" one of the EMTs asked. "Any pain around your neck or shoulders?"

Alicia shook her head slightly, then groaned and pointed to her legs. Stacy glanced over at the EMTs. "It's difficult to tell what's happening down there because of the dashboard in the way."

The other EMT snapped on a pair of gloves and moved in beside Stacy to slip his hands beneath the dashboard to feel around. When he pulled it back out again, his glove was covered in blood.

"Broken tibia at least. Maybe fibula, too."

He took off the soiled glove then dug in the med pack at his feet. "We'll give her something for the pain. Alicia, what have you had to drink?"

She mumbled something about just a few beers, and the EMT and Stacy exchanged a look.

"I'll radio it in," the first EMT said, heading back up the hill. "And I'll have the Air Vac ready just in case."

Stacy edged farther into the car so she could figure out how to get the victim out of there safely as the EMT packed gauze pads beneath the dashboard around Alicia's legs to help stem the bleeding. If they knew for certain the woman had no spinal injuries, they could feel safer examining her more thoroughly. But until they got a cervical collar on her and spinal boards down here, no way was Stacy going to risk paralyzing the woman.

A moan issued from Alicia, and Stacy glanced back at her face. Her lips looked slightly bluer than before. Never a good sign. She signaled for the EMT to check her breath sounds again.

"Definitely decreased," the guy said a moment later. "Especially on the right-hand side. Punctured lung, maybe, due to a broken rib from the steering wheel."

Trouble was they had no idea of Alicia's medical history, and the victim was in no proper state to tell them. Alicia started wheezing and gasping for breath, more than Stacy would have expected from a collapsed lung alone. Scowling, she eased out of the car and picked up the woman's purse again to find an inhaler. Yep, Alicia was asthmatic. She managed to get the inhaler into Alicia's mouth and administer the medication. "That's it. I'm going to give you a few puffs. I know it's hard to breathe when your chest hurts, but try to get as much air as you can, okay? That's it. You're doing great, Alicia. That should help a bit until we can get you out of there."

An hour later they'd managed to get the spinal board down to the crumpled vehicle, and between six cops, three firefighters and two EMTs, they eased the dashboard off Alicia's legs and got both her and the passenger out of the vehicle and safely back up the hill to the ambulance.

Stacy rode in the back of the rig to the hospital with her, mainly because Alicia refused to let go of Stacy's hand the entire way.

When they got to Key West General, the ER was swarming with people, as usual.

Luis met them at the door, looking about as haggard as Stacy felt after their dinner together two nights ago. "What have we got?"

She stayed by the gurney as the EMTs ran down the case and they wheeled Alicia down the corridor to an open trauma bay. Stacy kept her focus on the patient, even as she could feel Luis's stare burning a hole through the side of her.

"Patient's name is Alicia Myers. Twenty-seven. MVA near Higgs Beach. Jaws of Life used to cut her from the car. Cause of accident unknown at this point, but alcohol may have been a factor. Suspected fractured left tibia, possibly fibula as well. We gave her ten of morphine at the scene around an hour ago. Patient is also asthmatic and may have a right-sided pneumothorax. Her color has improved with omalizumab, but she's been struggling with her breathing since we came on scene."

Luis took over from there. "Let's get her set up in trauma bay three. We'll need a portable chest X-ray and a chest tube tray, please." He turned and locked gazes with Stacy for a long moment, then followed his nurses and staff

into the trauma bay and closed the curtain.
"Let's go, people. Time is life."

By the time Luis got his patient stabilized
and headed off to the OR with an orthopedic surgeon, several hours had passed. Alicia was expected to make it. She was a lucky
woman.

And speaking of lucky, Luis headed upstairs to check in on Reed, the firefighter
with the bad fracture. It had been four days
since his accident. Normally, when he passed
patients on to other physicians, that was the
end of his involvement. But Reed's case had
stuck with him, in no small part because of
Stacy.

Speaking of Stacy, he'd been unable to get
her or her son out of his mind, despite the
busy day. Correction. *Their* son. What did
he look like? Was he smart, funny, tenacious
like his mother? The only thing he knew for
certain was that the boy had inherited his
father's autism. He wanted to meet Miguel,
see for himself, but he didn't want to push
Stacy too far too soon. He didn't blame her
for not telling him before; he just wished he
hadn't missed so much time in his son's life.

Luis pushed out onto the ICU floor where
Reed's room was then walked down the

brightly lit corridor to the last door on the right. He knocked softly then stuck his head in to make sure he wasn't disturbing anything. Reed's wife spotted him and waved him inside, her smile kind and inviting.

"Dr. Durand, how nice to see you," she said, resuming her seat at her husband's bedside. "We weren't expecting you. Is everything okay?"

"Fine," he said, taking a chance to glance at Reed's file on the computer in the corner. "I'm on shift in the ER and there was a lull in cases, so I thought I'd pop up and see how things were going."

From what he could see in the file, the surgeon had been able to reestablish blood flow to Reed's leg. That was good news. The bad news was that leg had been without proper circulation for a significant period of time after the accident, which meant possible nerve and muscle damage that would only become evident as the days progressed.

"We're hanging in there, Doc," Reed said, taking his wife's hand. "Eager to get out of here and get back to work. When do you think that will be?"

Luis took a deep breath and faced the family. It was a tough conversation to have and not really his place. That was up to the ortho surgeon. But he could offer his opinion and hopefully set some realistic expectations. "Well, first off, considering your condition the last time I saw you, I'd say you're doing well. The fact you're up and talking with your family and laughing and smiling is good."

"But what about my leg, Doc?" Reed asked, his gaze pointed. "Give it to me straight. The ortho doc dances around the subject, but I want to know the truth."

"Right." Luis checked the file again then nodded. "This isn't my case anymore, but I'd say you have reason to be cautiously optimistic at this point. Once they get you started on physical therapy and up and around on that leg again, they'll be in a better position to give you a prognosis. It's important to keep in mind the severity of the injury and the amount of blood lost. Depending on how quickly you heal and how hard you work at regaining your mobility, there's a chance you can return to the fire department in some capacity."

"But not as a firefighter." Reed's voice held an edge of sadness. "I'm not sure I can sit behind a desk all day. I love being out in the thick of the danger, you know?"

Luis nodded. That adrenaline rush was

what had gotten the man into trouble to begin with, but he wasn't going to mention that now. "As I said, the orthopedic surgeon will have a better idea of prognosis. Be sure to bring up your concerns to him when he stops by next time to check on you."

"He's right, honey," Reed's wife said, kissing his fingers. "I'm just glad you're still here with me."

"Yeah." Reed frowned down at the sheets. "I just wish everything wasn't so up in the air."

"How are you feeling?" Luis asked, changing the subject.

"Like crap."

"But you're alive," his wife countered. "Do you remember any more about the accident?"

Reed sighed, sagging back into his pillows. "I remember everything."

Before Luis could ask him more about that, a couple of teens walked into the room, sidling past Luis to their dad's beside. A girl and boy who looked maybe fifteen and sixteen, respectively. No sign of the third kid yet. The girl was crying as she leaned carefully over the bed to cuddle into her dad's uninjured side.

"Dad, I missed you so much," the girl said, sniffling.

"I missed you, too, baby," Reed said, kissing the top of her head then looking over at Luis. "You got kids, Doc?"

He'd been about to answer no but stopped himself. That wasn't true. Not anymore. His pulse kicked up a notch as he gave a curt nod, saying for the first time, "Yes, a son. His name is Miguel."

"Aw, that's great." Reed's wife stood to move toward him. "Got any pics?"

"What?" He didn't have any pictures of Miguel. Not yet. Someday, though, he vowed to fill his entire memory with images of his son. Until then, he fudged a bit. "No. New phone. Haven't transferred them yet."

"Next time." Reed's wife went back to her seat, while their son slouched against the wall to check his phone. "They can be a handful, that's for sure. But so worth it. Right, honey?"

"Totally." Reed grinned, hugging his daughter tighter. "And because of them, I've promised never to ride another motorcycle again. Life's too precious to take those kinds of risks."

Luis chatted with them a bit more before heading back down to the ER. He liked to stay busy when things were slower, so he did busy work, like charting or inventory. Perhaps he'd do some of that tonight, since he'd already prepped the staff for the upcoming tropical storm. They'd just gotten a shipment of supplies in today, in fact, so maybe he'd help the orderlies put that away. It had been a long time since he'd done that kind of thing, but physical labor always helped clear his head, and Lord knew he could use some of that tonight with everything else going on.

He pushed out of the stairwell door, intending to head toward the supply closet at the end of the hall when he found his path blocked by the very woman who'd been foremost in his thoughts all day.

Stacy looked flushed and tense, and the hairs on the back of his neck rose at the fear in her eyes.

"What's wrong?" Luis asked, concerned. "What's happened?"

"It's Miguel—he's hurt," she said, the tiny catch in her voice tearing at his heart. "They've got him in trauma bay one."

They rushed toward the nurses' station and around the circular desk to the treatment area closest to the door. Luis didn't hesitate at all, just swished aside the curtain and rushed into the exam room with Stacy by his side. He had no idea what to expect. Blood, gore, some horrific disfigurement.

What he saw was a small boy with dark hair and wide brown eyes clutching a stuffed bear in his right arm while a nurse carefully treated his left one. Tears shone on the little boy's cheeks beneath the bright overhead lights. From the bruising and swelling on his left forearm, Luis quickly surmised he'd broken it. He turned to Stacy. "What happened?"

"I took him to the park near our apartment after I got off work today. It was nice out, and I thought it would be good to get some fresh air. My mom usually watches him, but she's up in Miami now visiting a sick friend before the storm hits. Anyway, Miguel was climbing the play set when I called hello to a friend from the complex, and his foot slipped and he fell."

She closed her eyes. "It's my fault. If I'd just waited until he was done before calling out…" Stacy sighed and shook her head. "I know it's not serious, but when I saw him lying on the ground, screaming and crying, holding his arm, it felt like my own heart was ripped out of my chest."

"Dr. Durand," the resident handling

Miguel's case said as he sidled past Luis. "You want to handle this one?"

He did, very much. But that would be a conflict of interest, so he couldn't. He fisted his hands at his sides, feeling none too steady himself at the moment. "No. You go ahead."

"Okay." The resident smiled down at little Miguel as he took a seat on his stool and wheeled into position near the side of the bed. "All right, buddy, I'm going to examine your arm now. It might be uncomfortable, but I promise it will be over quickly. Okay?"

Miguel gave a tiny nod, his little chin quivering. Luis wanted to rush over and gather the child in his arms, but that was impossible under the circumstances, so he stayed put, stomach churning and throat tight.

"He's very brave." Luis bent closer to whisper to Stacy, inhaling her sweet, floral scent and finding it calmed his nerves a bit. "Poor guy."

For a moment, she just stared at her son. Then, finally, she glanced up at him. "He's the best little boy in the world."

Luis believed her. Then Miguel whimpered slightly as the resident pressed a sore spot, and Luis's chest imploded. Pulse thudding, he turned away to check the boy's chart, needing something to occupy himself so he didn't act foolish and do something crazy like tell the boy who he was right then and there. He needed to speak with Stacy again, discuss how and when they'd let Miguel know about him. He wanted to be a part of this.

Needed to be a part of this.

A nurse stuck her head in to say, "Radiology is ready for him upstairs, Doc."

"Thanks," the resident said over his shoulder. "Okay, folks. We need to take him up to the third floor for some scans so we can set this bone properly. They're usually running a little behind, so it could take up to an hour." He reached down and ruffled Miguel's hair, and Luis felt a stab of jealousy.

"I'll stay with him the whole time," the nurse promised.

Stacy started to object, but Luis took her arm. Given their crazy schedules and the coming storm, this could be the last chance they had to discuss their son. "Let them handle it. We need to talk."

She looked like she wanted to argue with him, but then she exhaled slowly and glanced at the nurse. "Fine." Then she walked over to kiss the top of Miguel's head. "This nice lady is going to go upstairs with you okay, honey? Mommy will be waiting right here for you when you're done."

Miguel nodded, retuning his attention to what the nurse was doing beside him, seemingly fascinated by the details of her prepping the tray for the doctor to put on his cast.

The techs arrived a few minutes later, and they stepped out of the room. While they maneuvered Miguel's bed from the trauma bay, Luis whispered, "This wasn't how I expected to meet my son for the first time."

"No." Stacy tucked her hair behind her ear, then crossed her arms. "I still haven't said anything to him yet. Not until we know what we're going to do going forward."

"He's going to find out about me sooner or later." Luis frowned. "He has a right to know. I have a right to get to know my son. I don't want to fight over this, but…"

"I know." She held up a hand to forestall him. "I know. I just… It's hard for me."

"And you think it's not for me?" He did his best to keep the rising tension curdling inside him from his voice. Took a deep breath and started again. The last thing he wanted right now was to get into a fight with Stacy. They were both under a lot of pressure, and that could make you say or do things you'd regret later. Luis had enough regret for a lifetime already. They needed time to cool off and space to think clearly. "Look, this is important, and we need to plan out what we're going to say. Together. He'll be gone for a while for his scans. Perhaps we can grab a coffee in the cafeteria while they do that?"

Stacy hesitated then nodded, her stiff shoulders slumping. "Fine. Yes. Let me stay with him until they go upstairs. I don't want Miguel to be alone right now."

"Agreed." The boy had seemed okay earlier, but that could change fast depending on his condition and how he handled the discomfort of the casting process. Luis's chest constricted as they stepped out of the waiting room and back into the trauma bay. Miguel's eyes were red and Luis felt an unexpected urge to hug the boy and protect him, tell him everything would be all right. Those emotions were quickly followed by a bone-deep fear that his son could've been hurt even worse and how in the world would Luis ever keep him safe? Working in the ER, he'd dealt with his fair share of worried, distraught parents, but he'd never truly understood what they were going through until now. The feeling of helplessness, the overwhelming desire to do whatever was in his power to protect his son no matter what. He'd known the boy was his for barely forty-eight hours, and already the bond he felt to his son was strong.

Finally, the techs got the bed out into the hall and headed toward the elevators. Stacy was at Miguel's side, holding his right hand and whispering things to him to make him smile. His heart pinched with joy when Miguel smiled at him and held out his bear to Luis.

"His name is Dozer," the boy said, his expression serious. "They said I can't take him to the scans, so I want you to look after him until I get back. Don't let anything happen to him, Dr. Durand."

"Never," Luis vowed, taking the bear and grinning. The boy's hair was dark and curly, like his own. "And since we're friends, why don't you call me Luis?"

"Friends?" Miguel asked, brown eyes wide. "Are we?"

"I'm guarding Dozer. If that's not a friend, I don't know what is. Right, Mom?"

Stacy watched him closely for a second, then stepped back to allow one of the techs to get past her to steer their son's bed onto the elevator. "Right. Are you sure you don't want me to go with you, honey?"

"No. I'm a big boy now." Miguel shook

his head and pointed at the tech. "And she said she'll give me a treat when I'm done."

The tech grinned. "Sure thing."

They rolled Miguel away and Luis waited until the elevator doors closed and he and Stacy were alone again. He tucked Dozer safely in the pocket of his lab coat, then said, "Let's grab that coffee."

CHAPTER FIVE

"I WANT TO tell Miguel," Luis said, once they were sitting across a small table from one another in the cafeteria's glass atrium. "Today, before you leave the hospital."

"I thought we were going to talk about this first. Decide how it should be done." She was still trying to get her thoughts in order about him reappearing in their lives, let alone becoming a father to Miguel. Her mouth dried and her heart thudded hard against her rib cage. "I don't want to overwhelm him..."

"I know." Luis shook his head. "And I won't. I just want to get to know him a little, tell him who I am. With the storm coming and everything else going on, I believe we need to do this now. I want to tell my parents, too."

Stacy held up a hand and exhaled slowly. "Wait a second. This is all moving very fast."

"Yes. And I'm sorry for that, but that's

the situation we're in, Stacy, so we need to go with it. If anything happens to any of us during the storm…" He shook his head and stared down at the table. "Well, I don't want to take that chance and leave things unsaid."

The hint of sadness in his voice intrigued her far more than was wise. They still had so much to learn about each other, about their pasts. His pained expression told her now was not a good time to ask, though. Besides, she was too antsy, checking her watch frequently to make sure she didn't miss her son returning to his room in the ER. This was the first time she wasn't there by his bedside, and it felt wrong. She shook that off and concentrated on the conversation at hand, needing reassurance. "What are you going to say to him? His autism makes things a bit different. Maybe I can help you choose your words. Or I could be there when you tell him."

"I don't know." Luis toyed with his barely touched paper coffee cup. "But I think we should decide ahead of time. And when I do tell him, you should stay close, in case I get in trouble."

Oh, she'd stay close all right. Stacy watched him a moment then sat back, doing her best to quell the rising tide of dread inside her and failing. Luis was a good man. She knew that from what she'd seen of him and from what she remembered of their long-ago night together. He was hardworking, decent, kind, fair and true. But he was also an unknown factor here, and Stacy very much needed all her ducks in a row. "Look, Luis. Tell me honestly. Are you going to tell Miguel you're his father then disappear on him? Because if that's your plan, I'll need to do some damage control with Miguel. I don't want him getting attached only to be devastated later."

Luis looked at her, his dark eyes so similar to her son's it made her heart hurt. God, he was handsome, even after hours on a shift that had left him a bit rough and ruffled. He seemed so raw and vulnerable now that it made her feel like she'd kicked a puppy or something. But she'd lived through the pain of loving a dad so much only to have him walk away and never return, the pain of growing up without a father. She'd do anything in the world to keep her son from experiencing that. She'd taken a risk telling Luis about Miguel, and yes, he had a right to know. But if he betrayed the trust she'd put in him now, then…

Breath held, she waited for his response.

Finally, he said, "No. I'm not going anywhere. My traveling days are done. My plan is to begin a relationship with Miguel that will last a lifetime. But I need you to be patient with me. I've never done this and have no clue how to go about it. For a guy who is a stickler for rules and details, this is scary and maddening for me, but I'm doing the best I can here. You said Miguel knows nothing about me?"

The pressure in her chest easing a bit, Stacy took a deep breath then nodded. "No, not really. I mean, he's asked some questions. But more in a general sense than anything else. He noticed all his friends had dads around from time to time, even the ones with divorced parents. He wanted to know where his daddy was. I said you were helping people around the world, in far-off countries. So, not a total lie." She gave a small smile. "Anyway, one lesson you need to learn is to tell kids only what they want to know. Miguel never asked who you were, just where. That was a few months ago. Then I saw you in the ER that day, and now here we are."

"Hmm." He sipped his coffee then winced. "I wish you'd found me earlier."

"I tried, like I said. But working in Miami made it harder to make it down to Key West all that often. When I took the job here last year, I started asking around again, but things were busy at the department and with my mom moving down here with us, I was getting her stuff transferred and settled, too, and I just expected I'd have more time to work it all out."

"Is that all?"

"Yes." Defensiveness prickled up her skin, hot and uncomfortable. "I never intended to keep Miguel from you. Honest. You were gone when I first asked and things got so busy, and maybe I didn't want to face it at first, with what I'd been through in my past. And the longer it went on, the angrier I figured you'd be and the more confused Miguel would get and—" She threw her hands up in exasperation. "Things were complicated enough as it was. And if I told you and you didn't accept it, didn't want to acknowledge him as yours then—"

"Not acknowledge him?" Luis repeated, clearly confused.

Her spine stiffened, and she sat up straighter in her seat. "We had a one-night stand, Luis. It was hardly a committed relationship. And I didn't want you to think I was trapping you, that I wanted anything from you. It wouldn't have been completely out of left field for you to say you didn't want him or say he wasn't yours. Happens way more often than you think."

"No." Luis took her wrist, his hold gentle but firm. Tingles of awareness spread like wildfire through her system from his touch despite her wishes. He sat forward, closing the distance between them, close enough that she could see the hint of dark stubble just below the surface of his firm jaw, could feel the warmth of his breath on her skin, could smell his scent—soap and sandalwood. "It might have been just one night, but it meant something to me. I keep remembering that night between us…" His voice trailed off, and he shook his head at her inquiring look.

He thinks about me? About that night?

Lord knew she'd thought about that night, too, over the past five years, his tender touch, his heated words, his kisses and moans and the way he'd felt against her, within her…

No. This wasn't about that. This was about Miguel. Period. Amen.

She shifted slightly in her seat and crossed her legs away from him. "Go on."

"I believed you from the moment you told me about our son. And now that I've seen him, there's no denying he's mine. None. Miguel is my son." His hold on her wrist loosened, and he sat back a little. "Stacy, there are many things we still have to work out between us, about the past, but that doesn't have anything to do with what I need to work out with Miguel. If we can keep the two things in separate corners for now, it will make things much easier. I don't want to hurt Miguel because of things between us. That wouldn't be fair."

She swallowed hard against the unwanted lump of need in her throat and resisted the urge to rub her wrist. The old attraction to him still simmered inside her, even after all these years, but she forced it onto the back burner. "No," she said after a few tense seconds. "I suppose it wouldn't."

"So, I'll talk to him after he gets back from radiology." Luis looked up at her, his dark gaze unreadable. "Is that all right? Or should we do it together?"

Stacy gave a small nod. "I think that would be best."

Luis seemed to consider that a moment then shrugged. "Okay. Maybe you can tell him you were surprised to see me, which is true. Then I'll tell him that from now on, I'll always be around and he'll always know where I am. Sound good?"

"I guess." Her words sounded uncertain to her own ears, but she couldn't help it.

"Hey." He reached across the table again, this time taking her hand in his. His fingers felt strong and sturdy intertwined with hers. It felt right, which only made her nerves flare higher. He rubbed small circles on her palm with his thumb, his tone soft and soothing. "I know this is hard, but we can do this."

Her gaze met his and she wanted to believe him—boy, did she want to. "Okay."

"Okay." His phone vibrated in his pocket and he pulled it out with his free hand to frown down at the screen. "Looks like Miguel's done in radiology. We should get back up to the ER."

Luis stood in the doorway of the trauma bay while the resident finished up with Miguel's cast. The nurse who was assisting stood nearby with a tray of tools, chatting with the boy about what they were all for. Miguel seemed completely engrossed with it all. That was the Asperger's. Luis had had the same focus on details growing up. Still did.

Miguel looked a bit perkier now that they'd given him some meds for the pain and his arm was set. Still, in his shorts and brightly colored striped T-shirt, he looked very small in the large hospital bed. His dark hair was hopelessly rumpled and his cheeks were flushed, but he wasn't crying anymore, which was good.

The resident finished and stood, wheeling his stool back into the corner, and the nurse cleared out with the tray of instruments, leaving just Luis and Miguel and Stacy in the room. He took out the boy's teddy bear and handed him back safely to his owner.

"Safe and sound," Luis said, smiling.

"Thanks, Dr. Durand," Miguel said, hugging the beloved toy close. "I missed Dozer."

"He's a very good bear." Luis stood beside the bed.

"He helps me sleep."

"I bet he does." Luis couldn't hold back a grin even though his heart was lodged in his throat. "Do you mind if I sit down for a while?" he asked, pulling over the hard plastic chair near the wall and catching Stacy's eye. She gave him a tiny nod. It was time. "I'd like to ask you a couple questions, if that's okay."

Miguel blinked at him, dark eyes huge and serious in his small face. "Okay."

Blood racing, Luis took a deep breath. He'd had difficult conversations with patients' families that were easier than this. It felt like his entire future hung in the balance.

He needed to get this right. "Um, I wanted to talk to you about your daddy."

The little boy scowled at Dozer, straightening the bear's bow tie. "My daddy is across the world."

"Is that what Mommy said?"

"Yes." Miguel nodded, his brows knit as he glanced up at Stacy. "He helps people. He's a good daddy."

Luis's chest constricted. "What if I told you your daddy was here, now?"

The boy shrugged in response.

"Miguel." All the oxygen seemed to evaporate from the room, and time slowed. "I'm your daddy."

His son looked over at him then up at Stacy, not appearing incredibly impressed, and Luis's gut sank. "Where are your people?"

"The people I help?" Luis asked, connecting the dots of their odd talk. "Here, in this hospital. I help the people here in Key West now instead of traveling the world. I run this ER."

"Oh." That seemed to resonate a bit more with Miguel. "Can you get me another sucker?"

Stacy chuckled then bit her lip at his look. "Sorry."

Luis hid a smile of his own. "I'll see about having one sent over from the gift shop. What's your favorite flavor?"

"Raspberry."

"Mine, too," Luis said. "I'll tell the nurses as soon as we're done."

Miguel nodded then went back to fiddling with his bear. His purple and white cast stood out sharply against his tanned skin. "Do you want to sign this?"

It took Luis a second to realize he was talking about the cast. "Of course. Does it hurt?"

"Not really. Feels weird, though." The little boy frowned again then met Luis's gaze. "Do you have a dog?"

"No." Luis didn't have time for pets. He barely spent any time at all at his house. Which was a shame, since he'd had it built specifically to his designs the year prior, and it was lovely. Lots of glass and steel and lush landscaping. Even a pool. He imagined his son there now and suddenly couldn't wait to invite him and Stacy over. "I don't have a dog. Do you?"

"Not yet. Mommy's working to get me one, though, from her friend Lucy. She's a trainer."

"Nice. You must be excited."

"I am," Miguel said, his tone flat. "Do you have a grandma?"

Luis's gut tumbled a bit at that reminder of his past. He'd taken that fateful boat ride with his birth parents at six, but he could still vaguely remember his Cuban grandparents. Both sets of parents of his adopted parents had passed away before Luis had become part of their family. He swallowed hard. Now wasn't the time to get into all that yet, so instead he said, "I used to. When I was your age, I had a grandma and a grandpa. *Abuela y abuelo.*"

He braced himself for more hard questions, but they never came.

Instead, Miguel switched subjects entirely. "Did you know there is a hurricane on the way?"

"Yes." The knots between Luis's shoulder blades eased. "Hurricane Mathilda. Your uncle, Jackson, is actually running the team to handle the recovery efforts."

"Mommy's on that team, too. A typical hurricane can dump six inches to a foot of rain across a region. The most violent winds and heaviest rains take place in the eye wall, the ring of clouds and thunderstorms closely surrounding the eye. Every second, a large hurricane releases the energy of ten atomic

bombs. Hurricanes can also produce torna-
does."

"That's very impressive," Luis said, pride
over his son's memory swelling inside him
like a balloon. Luis himself had a near-
eidetic memory. It was both a blessing and
a curse. "Did you know the word 'hurricane'
comes from the Taino Native American word
hurucane, meaning evil spirit of the wind?
The first time anyone flew into a hurricane
happened in 1943 in the middle of World
War II. And a tropical storm is classified as
a hurricane once winds go up to seventy-four
miles per hour or higher."

Miguel narrowed his gaze on his father.
"Is that true?"

"Of course. I would never lie to you,
mijito." That last word sent a warm rush
through Luis he'd never experienced before.
My son. They continued chatting for a while
about storms and bears and even the Florida
Keys. Luis lost track of time as the last of his
tension drained away. It had gone well. He
was still glad to know Stacy was right there
and thought he was getting along pretty well
for a man new to all this.

Then Miguel yawned and asked Luis to
read him a story. They kept some children's
books at the nurses' station, so Stacy went

out and got one, letting the staff know that the room would be occupied a little longer. Thankfully, they weren't that busy at the moment, so it wasn't a problem.

Stacy returned and closed the door behind her then handed the book to Luis. He started to settle back in his chair, but Miguel insisted he sit beside him on the bed because that's how his mommy always did it.

Right. Luis wrestled with the bedrails and got them lowered, then stretched out beside his son's smaller form while Stacy took a seat in his vacated chair. The boy snuggled into his side, warm and wonderful, and rested his head on Luis's chest, his bear tucked beneath his cast. If Luis died right then and there, he'd be a happy man.

The longer he read about dogs in race cars and mermaids on buses, the more Luis realized he was tired. Exhausted, really. He hadn't slept well since reconnecting with Stacy, filled with stress and recriminations and what-ifs. Miguel fell asleep halfway through the second book, and Luis wasn't far behind.

"Luis," a voice said, followed by a shake of his shoulder.

He awoke slowly and it took a second for him to remember where he was. The hospital. Miguel's room. His son's room. Luis yawned and stared up at Stacy. So lovely. He smiled. Looked down at Miguel's dark head still snuggled on his chest then bent and kissed it. "How long was I asleep?"

His voice sounded groggy to his own ears.

"About half an hour," she said, helping him extricate himself from the bed without waking Miguel. "They need us to clear out so they can use the room for incoming cases."

"Oh, right." He yawned and stretched, then straightened his lab coat while she stacked the books he'd read and set them on the counter. At least things between them didn't seem quite so strained anymore, which was good.

Luis straightened his hair and clothes in the mirror over the sink in the room.

Stacy caught his gaze in the reflection. "I should wake Miguel so we can go."

Before he could stop himself, Luis turned to face her. "Have dinner with me. Just the two of us. There's still so much we need to talk about, and I'd like us to be friends." At her cautious look, he added, "For Miguel."

Stacy looked from him to their son, then back again. "I don't know. I'm super busy with the response team and then we've got a new recruit class getting ready to graduate at the fire station, and I teach a couple of classes on Monday and Thursday for the corps and I've got my captain's paperwork to catch up on in the afternoons. And that doesn't include my regular shifts with the fire crew. And I'll need to check with my neighbor since my mom's in Miami right now, and I'm just so busy and I—"

"Please. Come on. You have to eat, right? And we need to plan some things."

She winced and shook her head. "I don't know. I'm not sure that's such a good idea after what happened between us."

He frowned. "What? When?" Then it dawned on him. "You can't mean that night on the beach. I'm not going to seduce you again. It's just dinner."

Of course, now that he'd brought it up, seducing her seemed to be the only thing he could think about, but no. That was wrong. They had a son now, important matters to talk about. He needed to concentrate on that, no matter what his body might want.

Stacy was quiet a moment, staring down at her toes. Then she met his gaze, her blue eyes large and soft, full of conflicting emotions—anger, anticipation, anxiety, wary hope. "Look, Luis. I really need you to hear what I'm about to say. You've been back in my life less than a week, and you've known about Miguel for even less than that. I'm glad you two have connected, but our situation doesn't change just because we made a child together."

"Miguel deserves a mother and a father," he said, keeping his voice low so as not to wake the boy.

"And he has them," she answered. "No matter what happens with us, we are his parents. But let's not rush ahead and make mistakes we might both regret later."

Frustrated, he raked a hand through his hair, disheveling it again, but he couldn't care less at the moment. "So, what the hell are we supposed to do, then? I thought planning out custody and finances and all that was what I should be doing."

"It is, but..." Stacy shook her head and pulled him into the corner farthest from the bed. "You still don't get it, do you? I don't want you in Miguel's life because you're doing what you think you should. I want you in his life because you love him and want to be there. He's your son, I won't get in the way of that, but I want you to consider what I've said carefully."

"Consider it? Hell, it's all I've thought

about since that night at the pub." Luis stood there a second, staring at her, until finally he said, "Look, I'm not going anywhere. I don't know what I need to do to convince you of that, Stacy, but whatever it is, I'm determined to try. I know your father hurt you deeply when he left, but please don't punish me for his mistakes. Please. I'd like to come over tomorrow after you get off work and spend some time with Miguel, if that's acceptable. Will you trust me enough to do that?"

Without thinking Luis reached over and put his hand on the back of her neck, running his thumb from her earlobe to the base of her throat, remembering she'd liked that before and hoping it soothed away some of the tension from her beautiful face. Then he leaned in and kissed her. Light, sweet, fast.

They both blinked. She looked as stunned as he felt.

Heat prickled his cheeks and he let her go. "I...uh... I..."

"Mommy?" a small voice said from the bed. "What are you doing?"

Stacy blushed and looked past him to their son. "Daddy and I were just talking. Are you ready to go home?"

While she went over to collect him, Luis

leaned a hand against the wall, scrubbing the other over his face. *What the hell am I doing?* Kissing Stacy was not going to help the situation, but that seemed like all he wanted to do at the moment. He was a man ruled by science, facts, details, service to others.

But at the moment, the emotions roiling inside him felt every bit as dangerous and disturbing as the hurricane headed their direction.

CHAPTER SIX

THE NEXT DAY, the only thing that surprised Luis more than how easy it had been to fall into a routine with Miguel was how readily the boy had seemed to take to him. It shocked him to realize how much he looked forward to spending time with his son.

In fact, as soon as his shift was over, he headed for Stacy's apartment, as promised. According to his watch, she should have just arrived home after her shift as well. She answered the door wearing a loose, comfy-looking sweat suit, her hair still damp from the shower.

"Hey," he said. "Looks like I'm right on time. Okay if I come in?"

She stepped aside to let him in. "Yes."

"Tough day?"

"I expected it to be slower at the station, but nope." She closed the door then brushed past him, the sweet scent of her shampoo surrounding him as she passed. "One run after another all day long. I'm exhausted, honestly."

"Then rest. Why don't you take a nap?" He smiled. "I can take Miguel to the park and with me while I run some errands while you sleep. Would that be acceptable?"

"Oh. I…" She frowned then yawned, dark circles marring the delicate skin beneath her eyes. "I don't know. You've not been alone with him yet. Not for any length of time, and he can be a handful and—"

"Please?" Luis stepped closer and took her hand. "I'm an ER doc. I deal with difficult patients every day. I think I can handle one four-year-old boy. I promise I'll take good care of him, and I'll call you if any issues arise." He placed his other hand over his heart as a sign of sincerity. "Please trust me?"

She seemed to consider that a second then glanced at the clock. "Two hours. That's it. Then I want you both back here. And don't let him talk you into buying him a bunch of junk food. I'm making dinner. Mom's still in Miami, so it's just us."

"Sounds good. And thank you. I'll take good care of our son, I swear." He grinned, more relieved than he could say. "Now, where's Miguel?"

"Daddy!" The boy called from down the hall then came running out to throw his arm around Luis's legs. The move made it a tad awkward to keep his balance, but he wouldn't change it for the world.

Stacy and Luis both looked at each other, shocked. Twenty-four hours after they'd just met for the first time and now he was Daddy. A small frisson of pleasure jolted through Luis from that title, and from Stacy's expression he saw some chasm between them had been crossed. Now there was no going back. Everyone had their assigned roles, and you didn't shirk a responsibility like that.

It was both the most complicated and simplest transition Luis had ever experienced. But the problem remained that he and Stacy still had not negotiated their relationship. They were still dancing around it and hadn't even mentioned their brief kiss in the trauma bay. Essentially, they were still two strangers, navigating these murky waters. And now there was one more person to consider. And that person was currently squeezing his leg like his life depended on it. Luis reached down and ruffled Miguel's hair like he'd wanted to do the day before, loving the silky feel of the kid's hair on his fingers.

"Hey, *mijito*. How are you?" he said, grinning down at the boy. "Want to go to the park with me?"

"Yes, please," Miguel said, stepping back to gaze up at him. "I'm ready."

"You need shoes first, mister," Stacy said, shooing him back toward his bedroom. "And socks."

Miguel grumbled but did as he was told.

Alone again, Luis turned back to Stacy. "Need anything at the store while we're out? Any advice?"

"No, nothing from the store. And advicewise, use his car seat even though he complains, wear seat belts, make frequent bathroom stops, never let him out of your sight. And come home safe. Both of you."

"Got it." He grinned.

"Good. And don't forget to call me with any problems. I'm a light sleeper, especially when I nap."

"Will do." He nodded, his expression serious now, thinking about all the things they had to discuss. If they'd had more time, or better weather on the horizon, it would've been easier to spread this stuff out. But with the storm strengthening each day and changing trajectory by the hour, everything seemed up in the air. And once an emergency declaration was made for the Keys, all their attention would need to be focused on the rescue and recovery efforts, and who knew where they'd stand after that, if they'd even be standing at all.

His phone buzzed in his pocket, and he pulled it out to check the screen.

"Anything important?" Stacy asked.

"No. Just a calendar reminder for the team meeting day after next."

"Right."

Miguel ran back down the hall, shoes and socks in place and Dozer tucked under his arm. "Ready!"

"Okay." Luis took his son's hand then walked to the door, speaking to Stacy over his shoulder. "Get some rest, Mommy. We'll see you later."

"See you," Stacy said, waving to them then walking down the hall to her own bedroom and shutting the door.

"All right, *mijito*," Luis said to his son. "How about we hit the park first then do some errands?"

"Okay, Daddy," Miguel said, tugging on his hand. "Ready."

Luis let them out of the apartment and

locked the door behind them. He hadn't lied
to Stacy about his experience dealing with
difficult patients, but honestly, they were
mostly of the adult variety. And while he
was sure those skills would translate to the
younger generation, the fact was he'd never
spent much time alone with kids as an adult.
When he'd been on his mission trips, it was
always busy and hectic and there wasn't
much time for socializing outside work. And
most of his free time now was taken up with
hospital functions and working at the pub,
so not many kids there, either. On the few
occasions where he'd been with friends who
had children, he'd fit in fine, tossing a ball
around or making faces and playing dolls or
whatever. But this was the first time he was
solely responsible for a child's well-being—
and that child belonged to him.

While they were at the park, Luis learned
something he'd never encountered before.
Apparently, a man with a child held some
extreme fascination and attraction to women.
He never really paid much attention to his
looks, though his brother, Jackson, was always teasing him about being a "chick mag-
net." Now, though, strange women came up
to him at the park, remarking on how cute
Miguel was and making small talk. They

kept asking him if he was having a father-son day or if he lived in the area and if they could set up a playdate for their kids sometime.

He refused them all, saying the first thing that came to mind, feeling extremely uncomfortable under the added scrutiny. "Thanks, but I have to get going. My wife is waiting."

Miguel tugged on his hand and asked, "Who's your wife, Daddy?"

The pregnant woman he was talking to gave Luis a look and he chuckled awkwardly, hurrying them out of there fast. On the way back to his car he said to Miguel, "We need to get our story straight, *mijito*."

They got in the car and started into town. Luis was feeling better about things until Miguel said out of nowhere, "Daddy? How do babies get in a mommy's tummy?"

Oh, Lord.

Guessing this had been brought on by the last conversation at the park, he slowed for a red light then turned to his son, hoping to change the subject. "How about if we stop and get some ice cream for dessert tonight after dinner?"

"Yes!" Miguel squealed. "Ice cream."

"What kind should we get?" he asked, glad for the reprieve. "Chocolate or vanilla?"

"Chocolate!"

* * *

Later that night, after dinner and chocolate ice cream, Miguel played in his room while Luis and Stacy did the dishes together in the kitchen.

"How'd it go today?" she asked, reaching up to put a plate on an upper shelf, the motion revealing a tempting swath of creamy skin at her lower back. Luis swallowed hard and looked away fast.

"Uh… Good. We went to the park then into town for a while." He laughed. "It was weird, because all these women kept coming up to me to chat. They even asked me for my phone number."

She stopped midway through putting away another plate and looked back at him over her shoulder. "Are you serious? They were propositioning you right there with my son standing by?"

"What?" Luis's face flamed hot, the flames licking down his neck to the open vee of his dress shirt. "No. They weren't propositioning me. They wanted to set up playdates."

"Uh-huh." Stacy lowered from tiptoe to flat foot, smirking. "I'm sure they wanted to play, all right."

He frowned, flustered. It hadn't been like that, had it? It didn't mean anything. He wasn't looking for that. Not with Miguel in his life now. And Stacy. If he wanted to become intimate with anyone again, it was her. Except he shouldn't be thinking like that. They'd had a nice dinner. Later, they'd have a nice chat. That was all tonight was about.

Isn't it?

The sound of blocks tumbling down echoed from the hall, followed by Miguel singing an off-key tune from one of his favorite children's shows on TV. Stacy tossed her towel aside. "I should check on him. Be right back."

After she returned, Luis told her about Miguel's question in the car. Stacy laughed so hard she had to lean against the counter as she doubled over.

"It wasn't funny," he said, perplexed. "What should I have said?"

"I have a special book all about that for him," Stacy said, wiping her eyes with her towel. "I guess it's about time we start reading that together. I'd put it off, thinking he wasn't ready yet, but apparently I was wrong."

He scrunched his nose. "They have books for kids his age about *that*?"

"No. Not about *that*, per se." She smiled at him. "It talks about the differences between mommy and daddy bodies. It's all very sweet and nonthreatening." She nudged him with her shoulder. "If you're good, maybe I'll read it to you later, too."

Relaxing a bit, he flirted right along with her. "Yeah? Well, maybe if you're very good, I'll give you a live demonstration."

Pretty pink flushed her cheeks, and she turned away to put away the rest of the dishes. "I remember how it goes, thanks so much."

So do I.

He bit back those words and took a deep breath, instead asking something that had been on his mind for a while now. "How did it happen in our case?" He waved a hand between them. "I mean, I know the mechanics of it, and we'd both had a lot to drink, which is probably why I didn't use a condom that night. That part's all a bit fuzzy, to tell you the truth."

She took a deep breath. "It's kind of fuzzy for me, too. But I do remember I'd messed up my pills a week or so before that night, so that didn't help, I'm sure. Things happen."

Silence descended for a short time. Then Luis couldn't resist and leaned forward to kiss her forehead. "Well, I'm not sorry about it. Miguel is awesome. Big accident, huge reward."

Stacy smiled then gave him a quick hug. Apparently, he'd managed to say the right thing for once since this whole thing started, and relief warmed him. "You've had a good time with Miguel, haven't you?"

"He's amazing. Seriously." He squeezed her back then stepped away. "But once we get him to bed, I do think we really need to talk about all this."

"You're right." Her expression shifted from joy to resignation. "I'll go get him changed into his pj's. He's probably finished building his skyscraper anyway."

Once Miguel was tucked in for the night and the lights were out, the apartment was still. Luis and Stacy sat on the sofa in her living room, two glasses of wine on the coffee table before them. They chatted quietly about their pasts, their families, their hopes and dreams and fears. All the things most people knew about each other before they hopped into bed together. For them, it was a revelation.

"That must have been terrible," she said, her voice rough with unshed tears as she pictured a little Luis alone in a strange, new country, orphaned, left to fend for himself.

It helped her understand him so much better. Why he worked so hard, why he went to such great lengths to help others, why he was so driven.

"They sacrificed everything to give me a better life," he said, staring down at his hands in his lap. "The least I can do is live my life in a way that makes them proud."

She couldn't resist reaching over and placing her hand over his. "I'm sure they're proud of you, Luis. Look at everything you've accomplished. They must be looking down on you from heaven and beaming with joy."

"I hope so." He took a deep breath then looked up at her. "What about you? What about your family? What happened to your father?"

Stacy flinched slightly then sat back, pulling her hand away from his. Luis frowned, but didn't reach for her. She picked up her wineglass then tucked her legs beneath her. "He left us when I was eight. Just packed up his stuff and walked out the door without so much as a goodbye. I haven't seen him since."

"I'm sorry."

"Why?" She snorted. "Wasn't your fault."

"No. But that must have hurt you very much."

"It's fine." She tried to shrug it off, as she always did. But with Luis watching her so closely, those deep, dark eyes of his filled with caring and concern, she felt an unexpected, nearly overwhelming need to let down her walls, to let him in, show him the wound inside her from her father's abandonment that hadn't healed, might never heal. Even all these years later, it felt like a great, gaping hole in her soul. But putting that into words, laying herself bare like that, terrified her. "I've had a good life despite it."

This time, Luis reached for her, twining his fingers with hers, so strong, so warm, so tempting. "You've worked very hard. You're very brave."

Stacy blinked hard, sipping her wine to swallow the lump of emotion in her throat. She had worked hard. Harder than most folks knew. "After he left, Mom and I had to move into government housing in Miami because we couldn't afford the house anymore. She worked three jobs just to make ends meet. As soon as I was old enough, I went to work, too. Saved enough money to put myself through college, determined to prove that I didn't need a father to be successful. To prove I was good enough." She squeezed her eyes shut, concentrating on his silent, supportive presence beside her. "Prove I was worthy."

Luis scooted a bit closer, bringing her hand to his lips to kiss the back of it. "*Mi sirenita*, you have nothing to prove. You are good enough. You are worthy."

My mermaid?

The nickname he'd given her fit, she had to admit, given how they'd found each other on a moonlit beach that long-ago night. The sweetness of it fractured the barriers around her heart a little more and made her smile. She leaned forward to set her wineglass on the table, untucking her leg from beneath her. "Well, that's nice of you to say. Harder to believe, though. I always feel like I'm fighting battles. At work, in the world in general, just to be taken seriously. Just to be treated as an equal."

Luis sighed, keeping hold of her hand, rubbing his thumb softly, soothingly over her knuckles. "I've never experienced what you're going through, so I can't say I truly understand, but please know I'm there to support you and Miguel any way I can. In fact, I plan to set up a special bank account tomorrow for Miguel with you as the trustee, to cover educational expenses for him, plus anything else that he might need as he grows.

I want you to use the funds as well, as you need, to be comfortable."

Stacy listened quietly, mind swirling with this new information. She'd known he ran the emergency medicine department at Key West General and expected him to be wealthy because of it, but his generosity was beyond her imaginings. After their long-ago night together, she'd sometimes imagined what he'd be like in everyday life. Back then, she'd pictured him as some kind of millionaire playboy superhero, roaming the world saving puppies and old people. But the reality of Luis Durand was so much better than anything she'd ever expected. Kind, loyal, smart, strong, sexy as hell.

She swallowed hard. Nope. Not going there. No matter how easy it would be at this moment. She didn't want to go back there again with him, because having Miguel changed everything. Made it more real, more important, more meaningful. And she didn't want to need Luis like that.

Do I?

She hung her head and pulled away from him, wary and uncertain. Old habits died hard. "I don't know about all this. I've built a good life here. We have this apartment and Miguel is settled. I like my job at the fire department. It's hard work, but it keeps me in shape and sharp. And my mother visits frequently, too, and watches Miguel for me while I'm at work. Changing all that now…"

"I know," he said softly.

"For as long as I can remember, it's always been just Mom and me. And now Miguel. She's my best friend. And she and Miguel are very close, too."

"I know that, too. When Miguel asked me about my grandparents…" He gave a sad little laugh, and she sat back, moving closer to him so their shoulders touched, needing his support and wanting to return it to him as well. "I'm not trying to rush anything. I just wanted to help take the pressure off you. I know it's only been a few days, but I thought things were going well so far."

Tears stung her eyes, and she looked over at him. "They have been going well. Very well."

Their gazes locked, and slowly, they leaned toward each other. Stacy held her breath, her eyes flickering down to his firm, full lips, remembering how they'd felt against hers, how he'd tasted that night on the beach—booze and pure, sinful decadence. Luis stopped a millimeter away, his breath fast like hers, giving her a choice, waiting for her consent.

In the end, there was no choice for Stacy. Want clawed inside her, demanding this kiss, this moment, this night with him. She desired him more than she'd thought possible, and tonight, she'd have him.

Stacy closed the tiny gap between them, kissing him softly at first, then harder as she licked his lips and he gasped. All at once, he took charge, one hand at the back of her head and the other at her waist, pulling her across his lap and holding her against him. When he pulled away at last, they were both breathless.

"Is this what they mean by coparenting?" he asked, his forehead resting against hers before he trailed his lips up her neck to her ear.

She giggled, sinking her fingers into his thick, dark hair. "Pretty sure that's a no. But we're a bit more than coparents anyway."

He pulled back slightly to flash a sly smile. "Are we? *Si.* I think we are, *mi sirenita.*"

They kissed and touched and cuddled on the sofa until their clothes got in the way, then by mutual consent they moved to her bedroom at the end of the hall, careful not to make any noise to wake Miguel.

Luis was the same considerate, caring, expert lover she remembered from their night together. She'd never been more grateful for his attention to detail than she was now. He started at her ankles and worked his way up, nuzzling and licking then making love to her with his lips and tongue and fingers. When she came apart in his arms, he kissed his way up her body then covered her mouth with his to swallow her cries of pleasure. He pulled a condom from his pants pocket and smoothed it on, then he was inside her once more, filling her, completing her in a way she'd only ever experienced with Luis.

He set up a rhythm, rocking slowly and gently, gradually building to an easy pace that had them both on the edge of ecstasy again all too soon. Stacy tried to hurry him, digging her heels into his buttocks, nails biting into his shoulders, into his hair, arching beneath him. She needed more, deeper, faster.

She whimpered. "Please, Luis. Please..."

Luis chuckled low, whispering Spanish endearments in her ear as his thrusts grew deep and powerful, hitting the right spot within her, and that was all it took. Stacy's world shattered into a million fireworks of pleasure. He whispered into her ear, *"El mar y el cielo se ven igual de azules y en la dis-*

tancia parece que se unen," then let himself
go with a low moan of pleasure.

For a long time after, they just lay there,
holding each other as they slowly floated
back down to earth. Finally, as he lay par-
tially atop her, his head resting between her
breasts and her fingers toying with his hair,
she asked, "What did that mean?"

"Hmm," Luis said lazily, raising up to
meet her gaze. He looked tired and tousled
and totally adorable. Her heat squeezed at
the picture they made.

You couldn't live in Miami without picking up some Spanish, but she'd been a bit
preoccupied and hadn't caught every word
he'd said at that crucial moment. "What did
you whisper right before…you know?"

His soft laugh ghosted across her skin,
raising goose bumps in its wake. He kissed
the side of her breast then smiled against
her skin. "It's a line from a song. I remember my mother singing it to me on our way
from Cuba. 'The sea and the sky look the
same blue, and in the distance, it looks like
they join.'"

Stacy blinked up at the ceiling, stunned.
Touched more deeply than she wanted to
say at the moment, she just lay there, strok-
ing Luis's scalp until he fell asleep. Did he

see this as a step toward something more? Did she?

She wasn't sure. She'd meant what she said before about being in a good place in her life. She was glad he and Miguel were getting along so well and wanted them to have a connection in the future, but was she willing to upend everything she'd worked so hard to build to start over again with Luis?

Maybe she was reading too much into it, like she usually did. He'd not mentioned anything about getting together with her, beyond taking care of Miguel. Maybe he didn't want a relationship, just the occasional hookup. Maybe he'd decide to go off to the other side of the planet again and leave them behind.

That last thought scared her most of all, and it took a long while, surrounded by shadows, before Stacy followed Luis into sleep.

CHAPTER SEVEN

STACY HAD THE next day off from the fire department but went in for a few hours that morning anyway to take care of some paperwork, leaving Miguel with Luis at her house. Her mother was still in Miami until the weekend, and Luis didn't have another shift in the ER until that night.

When Stacy walked into her apartment that afternoon, she encountered one of the biggest messes she'd ever seen. Newspapers spread over the island in the kitchen were covered in craft supplies. There were scraps of paper on the floor and glitter literally everywhere. In the center of it all sat a black backpack covered in hand-painted designs and bright sparkling handprints.

"Hey," Luis said, coming out of the bathroom down the hall, drying his hands on a towel. "You're home early. We were just getting Miguel's school supplies ready for September."

"Mommy!" Miguel shouted excitedly, running up to her from down the hall. "Look what Daddy and I made!"

"It was a bit awkward with him only having one hand and I think there's as much glitter on his cast as there is on the backpack, but…" Luis said, ruffling his son's hair with a wink.

"And on the floor," Stacy noted. "Please tell me you're planning on cleaning this up, too?"

"Of course." Luis leaned in and kissed her cheek. "Why don't you change and relax until I get this under control."

"Or I can change then come help. Glitter is notoriously hard to get rid of." She went to her bedroom and returned two seconds later. "There's a duffel bag in my bedroom."

"Uh, yeah," Luis said, looking up at her from where he was stooped over, dustpan in hand, grinning. "I thought I might stay the rest of the week. Until your mother returns."

She stared at him, speechless.

He set his broom and dustpan aside and walked over to her, taking her arms gently, his expression serious. "Look, I'm sorry I didn't ask, but after last night, I thought…"

He looked away then shook his head. "I'm sorry. I should have run it by you first, but I thought it might be more convenient for both of us if I'm here. With the storm coming soon and me over here all the time as it is, I can take babysitting shifts when you're at work to fill in for your mother, and I promise I'm neat and won't get in the way. Can I stay?"

Her heart thudded hard against her rib cage and she wanted to say yes, but that small niggle of doubt was still there in the background. "Uh, we've never really done this before." She gestured between them. "Living together."

Luis's dark gaze turned tender, and her knees tingled. "First time for everything."

True. And it wasn't like this was long term or anything. No need to get too flustered about it. It was a couple of days at most. And he was right. It would be easier with them all together through the storm. They had another team meeting tomorrow, and with her mom gone, she did need to arrange care for Miguel when she wasn't home, so...

"Okay," she said at last.

He gave her a quick kiss then returned to his sweeping while she went back to the bedroom to change. By the time she came back out, Luis had the kitchen cleaned and he was starting dinner. Thick pork chops in a marinade. He looked back at her over his shoulder as he worked near the stove. "Better?"

"Yes, thanks. Where's Miguel?"

"In his room, playing with his new backpack."

She walked to his side and hugged him around the waist. "Thanks for that."

"No problem." He put an arm around her and pulled her into his side, whispering in her ear, "Hope you don't mind if we eat a little earlier, since my shift at the hospital starts at eight."

"Fine with me," she said, kissing his neck then stepping away. "What can I do to help?"

It all felt very domestic and normal and safe.

Stacy found herself liking it. A lot. Way more than she should.

They had a nice dinner as a family, then Luis excused himself to get ready for work while Stacy and Miguel did the dishes. Okay, Stacy did the dishes and Miguel mainly played in the bubbles, but still. After they were done, they sat in the living room together, watching a movie.

"Okay. I'm on for twenty-four, so I won't

see you again until the meeting tomorrow." Luis stopped by the sofa on his way to the door, kissing her on the cheek and Miguel on the top of the head. "Be good. Both of you. And call me if you need anything."

As she watched her son's cartoons on TV, Stacy ran through everything that had happened in the last few days. It was a lot. Too much, really, to process in such a short time. Miguel seemed to be dealing with it better than her, but his worldview and experiences of life were much simpler. Hers, on the other hand, were complicated with a capital *C*.

Part of her said Luis was great and she was lucky to have him. The other part of her, though, wasn't so sure. Honestly, the truth was, she wasn't good at asking for help or taking it when it was offered. Probably because she'd always been the helper. First with her single mother growing up, and now in her job and as a single mother herself. Her whole life, she'd always experienced that imbalance, more give than take, so her first instinct was always to handle things herself, to figure it out on her own. Self-reliance was her go-to mode.

Giving that up was hard, even when something that could be wonderful was at stake.

Restless, she got up and puttered around the apartment while Miguel finished his show. She took out the trash, looked through her emails, gave Miguel his bath, then put him to bed, reading with him until he fell asleep, his little mouth open like a tiny bird's. Even now, each time Stacy watched her son, she couldn't help thinking *He's mine!* It still filled her with wonder, with awe. Miguel was the miracle she didn't deserve.

About nine o'clock that night, she got a pint of ice cream out of the freezer and took a seat on the sofa again, clicking on the TV without really watching it as she checked her phone for text messages. Surprisingly, there was one from Luis already.

Did you find your surprise?

She chuckled and patted the pint of her favorite flavor of ice cream then texted back.

I did. Thank you. I think this live-in situation is working out just fine for now.

Right? Only took us five years to get here.

Her stomach knotted and she swallowed hard against the sudden constriction in her throat. She didn't believe Luis would run out on her and Miguel, but it had only been a few days. What would happen when things got tough? Miguel would start school next month, and even with him being in a special needs class, it was bound to be tough on him. Then there was the hurricane. If the weather reports were any indication, it was getting stronger, which meant increased chances of widespread flooding and damage. Both she and Luis would be on the front lines of search and rescue and recovery for the people of Key West. Could this, whatever this was between them now, survive the coming storm?

She wasn't so sure. There were still a lot of things to work out between them. Her phone buzzed again, and a new text popped up from Luis.

Still there? Something I said?

Torn and twisted, Stacy typed back a quick response then shut her phone off and stared at the TV without really paying much attention.

Sorry. Tired. Going to bed. Talk to you tomorrow.

* * *

Luis worked through the night, and luckily it was busy, keeping him from dwelling too much on Stacy's odd response to his text. The cases ranged from the usual cuts and broken bones to an allergic reaction to shellfish that had quickly escalated to anaphylaxis with the patient unable to breathe. He'd had to perform an emergency tracheostomy to clear an airway for the man, who was now recovering nicely in an overnight room after they'd pumped him full of Benadryl and epinephrine.

But as dawn drew closer, the new arrivals dwindled and Luis found himself thinking about Stacy and how well the last few days had gone. He wasn't a man prone to wild bouts of emotion—another side effect of his mild Asperger's—but when he did go off the deep end, he fell hard and fast.

He worried now that perhaps he'd become too invested in his relationship with Stacy too fast and scared her off. That was the last thing he'd wanted to do, but man. Miguel had definitely thrown him for a loop. Such a great kid. So much like Luis, but also with Stacy's fierce independent spirit.

Independence. Something he knew was very important to Stacy. And he would never want to infringe on that. He just wanted to be a part of their lives, if she'd let him.

That was a big *if* at this point, though.

Not that Luis could blame her.

In those moments when he could take a step back and look at the situation objectively, he knew things were moving fast. Maybe too fast. But then he also knew how quickly things could spin out of control and be snatched away from you. He never wanted to lose something precious to him again because he'd failed.

It was confusing and confounding and had him completely tied in stressful knots inside.

He took a break and went down to the cafeteria, forced down some tasteless eggs and toast, drank some much-needed coffee, then went upstairs to check on the firefighter, Reed. The guy was still in the hospital but had been moved from the ICU to a regular ward. He took the stairs up to the fifth floor and pushed out into the brightly lit corridor. The halls were bustling with carts of breakfast orders for patients in rooms, and the air smelled of bacon and oatmeal. Luis nodded to a few nurses and doctors he passed along the way then knocked on Reed's door at the end of the hall before entering.

It was a bit before 8:00 a.m., but patients

were up early at Key West General, what with their vitals being checked and physicians making rounds before going to their offices for appointments. Luis found Reed sitting up this morning in the chair by his bed, a tray of food on the table before him and a walker in the corner, near where his wife sat reading the paper.

"Good morning," Luis said, raising a hand in greeting. "Just thought I'd stop in again to see how you're doing."

"Morning, Doc," Reed said with a nod. "Doing well, thanks."

He hiked his chin toward the walker. "Looks like they've got you up and moving now?"

"They do." Reed chugged some orange juice then wiped his mouth with a napkin. "Surgeon said he did everything he could for my leg. Now it's up to me to finish what he started. After the accident, I didn't know how bad I was hurt. I mean, I knew it was bad, but not like this." He vaguely gestured to his lower half. "Anyway, at least I didn't lose my leg. The surgeon didn't think I'd walk again, but I'm not giving up until I try."

Luis admired the man's determination and grit. Seemed that was a prerequisite in their department, at least based on what he knew from Stacy. He'd meant what he'd told her before. She was one of the bravest people he'd ever met.

"Well," Luis said, "I'm sure with that attitude, you'll get much farther. Outlook is everything is some cases."

"Agreed." Reed bit off half a piece of bacon and chewed, grinning over at his wife. "People told me no way would I be using a walker yet, so I had to prove them wrong, didn't I, honey?"

His wife nodded from behind her paper, not looking up.

"They tell me I can't do something, that's the best way ever to make damn sure I do." He winked. "Most of us hose haulers are that way."

Luis bit back a laugh. "Excuse me? Hose haulers?"

Reed waved him off. "Nickname the cops had for us in the last blood drive. Friendly rivalry and all. I won't tell you what we called them." He winked again. "Anyway, like I said, I like being told I can't do something. Always been outgoing, crazy, up for anything, doing anything." With a sigh, his shoulders slumped. "But I'll tell you something. When I woke up after the surgery on my leg, found out the extent of what had hap-

pened, saw what I put my wife and my kids
and my crew through, I'm done. I won't ever
deliberately put them through that again."

"Sounds like a wise choice," Luis said,
leaning back against the wall behind him.
"Looks like you're recovering well."

"I'm doing good, Doc." Reed nodded.
"But my goal isn't just to walk. I want to
get back to work again, too. I know I've got
a ways to go, but I need that in my life. The
job's dangerous, I know that, but I help a lot
of people and that's what I enjoy most. Know
what I mean?"

"I do." His phone buzzed with a text from
the ER requesting him back downstairs. Luis
smiled at Reed and his wife. "Need to get
back downstairs. I'll try to stop in again before you're released to say goodbye."

"Goodbye?" Reed's wife glanced up at
him over the top of her paper. "From what
I heard, we might start seeing a lot more of
you around the fire department."

Luis froze in place, eyes wide. He and
Stacy hadn't told anyone about what was
happening with them, since it was so new.
They'd not really had a formal arrangement
about that, though. Had she said something
to her crew when she'd gone into work earlier? "Uh…"

Reed's wife grinned at his obvious discomfort. "I'm just teasing you. I've seen you and Captain Williams spending time together around the hospital, that's all. You're both single, so if something did spark between you then…"

"Leave the doc alone, Annette," Reed chided his wife. "Poor guy's busy. Let him get on with it."

Luis left quickly, feeling oddly like he'd just escaped a firing squad, and headed back down to the ER, glad for the cool air in the stairwell on his heated face.

The rest of the morning passed quickly, and before he knew it, it was time for the Emergency Response Team meeting. He was looking over the new films of Reed's leg postsurgery at the nurses' station when his brother, Jackson, walked in.

"Those for the motorcycle accident victim we brought in last week?" Jackson asked, checking out the scans of a badly fractured leg.

"Yes." Luis scrolled through several more images then clicked off the computer. "He's doing much better, according to the last report I got from the ortho surgeon. Took hours of surgery to repair all the damage. They're going to evaluate his leg today."

"That's tough, man. I know when we picked him up from the scene, there was a lot of gravel and denim and bits of bone we had to debride from the wound. I hope they can save it."

They walked out of the ER together and down the hall toward the conference room. From what Luis had seen from the weather reports on the TVs in the cafeteria earlier, Hurricane Mathilda had changed course yet again and Luis wondered if they'd be raising the readiness level in the area since the storm seemed to be on a trajectory to at least cause some damage in the area. From the tense look on his brother's face, Luis guessed that answer was yes.

They discussed Reed's case a bit more as he held the door for Jackson then followed him inside the large room, immediately searching out Stacy and spotting her seated at the table near several other firefighters. There was one seat still open near her, and he made his way over to it as Jackson headed for the podium at the front of the room.

"Hi," Luis said, as he slipped into his seat then frowned at Stacy's distant expression. Not cold, exactly, but not warm, either. Given her odd response to his text, he could only guess there was something wrong, but he had no idea what. Now wasn't really the time he could ask, either, with the meeting starting. Meanwhile his mind raced with horrible scenarios. Was it Miguel? Had something happened to his son? Or was it something he'd done that had offended Stacy? Had he overstepped the mark by moving himself into her apartment like that and she'd just not wanted to tell him earlier?

He was hardly an expert on relationships, and sometimes his issues made him not the best judge of social norms. Dammit. He scowled up at his brother as the meeting got underway.

"Right. Let's get started, then," Jackson said. He was two years younger than Luis and adopted as well, but they were closer than blood. "Thanks, everyone, for coming in. We've got a lot of new information to cover today, so best get to it."

Jackson waited for the hushed murmurs to die down then jumped right in. "Unfortunately, the news I have today isn't good. Based on the latest forecast models from the National Weather Service, Mathilda is expected to strengthen to a category four storm by tomorrow morning, and though it won't make direct landfall in the Keys, we are expecting the outer bands to cause significant storm surge and wind damages throughout the area as it passes by. Therefore, I'm raising our readiness level to one, effective midnight tonight. You all know how this goes and should have been expecting it."

"Tomorrow morning?" Luis shook his head in disbelief. There was still much left to do in the ER. "That's much sooner than originally expected. I thought it wouldn't hit until tomorrow evening at the soonest."

"Like I said, things have changed fast." Jackson took a deep breath. "And given the hurricane's current speed and trajectory, once it hits the Gulf of Mexico and the warmer waters there, it's going to be a monster. So I've already put out bulletins to the local media, per our ERT protocol. Everyone on the team quarantines in Key West until after Mathilda passes. All top-level protocols are now in place and emergency services mobilized. We are warning residents in the Keys to evacuate to the mainland now or find lodging within Key West proper for the duration of the event. Any questions?"

Stacy cursed under her breath. "This is bad. My crew needs to double up on prep to be ready by that time. And I tried to call my friend Lucy before I came here. You met her last week, but she's not answering her phone. I texted her and offered to drive up and bring her, but she said no. She told me once before that if a storm like this happened, she'd stay at her place and ride it out, but this is going to be worse than anything we've seen in a while."

Luis swiveled to face Stacy. He wanted very much to take her in his arms and hold her but didn't dare in the crowded room of their colleagues. Not until he knew where they stood. "Please don't worry. I'm sure everything's fine. Lucy's a veterinarian. Maybe she had an emergency case come up or something. She'll call you later, I'm sure." He took a deep breath and plunged ahead, knowing he needed to find out, but dreading it all the same. "*Mi sirenita*, I can tell something is bothering you. Please talk to me, tell me what's wrong so we can—"

Jackson made his way over to them. "Everything okay?"

"Not really." Stacy rubbed her crossed arms. "Lucy isn't here today. I offered to pick her up and drive her in, but she refuses to leave her compound."

Jackson looked a bit sick at that. "I'll call her and talk to her about it."

"I don't think it will do any good," Stacy said, her expression concerned. "She's determined to stay there and ride this thing out, but I think this one's going to be bad, Jackson. She's tough, but not that tough."

"No. You're right. She can't stay there by herself." Jackson scowled. "It's too dangerous."

"Well, good luck getting her to budge, brother," Luis said, scrubbing a hand over his face. He thought of the conversation he'd just had with Reed and his wife. "All she has to do is not answer her phone. People do what they want and what they think is best, no matter the danger or who they hurt in the process, even themselves."

Beside him, Stacy gave a pained gasp, and he realized too late that she must have interpreted his words to be about her. He wanted to tell her the opposite was true, but she'd already turned away to talk to one of her fire crew members and Jackson was still there, and… Dammit it all to hell and back.

Jackson's phone buzzed, and his brother's dour expression lit with hope for a second before dying away. Luis wasn't sure exactly what was happening there between his brother and Lucy Miller, but it was quite apparent to him that something definitely was. His brother tapped Stacy on the shoulder and told her to go ahead and brief her departments and that he'd handle Lucy. After she left, Jackson turned to Luis again. "Can you take over IC for me tonight after my shift ends?"

"What? Why?" Luis frowned, warning bells clanging in his head. "You aren't going to do anything reckless, are you?"

"No."

Luis had heard that tone many times before from his brother and knew it meant exactly the opposite was true. His pulse thundered as adrenaline flooded his system.

"I can't leave Lucy out there by herself." He rubbed his hand over the top of his short hair as they made their way back toward the ER and the ambulance bay. "Look, the level one doesn't go into effect until midnight. If I drive out to Big Pine Key after my shift at nine, I'm sure I can get her and get back to Key West in plenty of time."

Yep. Reckless as hell. Luis gave him a look. "That's cutting it awfully close. No. I don't like it, Jackson."

"Well, good thing it's not up to you, then." Jackson dug in his heels. The brothers rarely fought, but when they did, it was usually over a matter of principle. "Look, I'm the one taking the risk here, okay? And I'm fine doing it." Luis gave his brother a dubious stare, and Jackson's expression hardened with anger. "Stop glaring at me like that. Really, it's fine. And this has nothing to do with sex, if that's what you're thinking. Lucy barely tolerates me. But as IC I can't just leave her out there to die, can I? Besides, she's disobeying my orders already by not being at the meeting. If I let her continue to do that I won't be seen as an effective leader, will I? So yeah. I'm going out there to get her."

"So, this is about the promotion then?" Luis asked, thoroughly unconvinced.

"Of course it is," Jackson said, throwing up his hands. "What else would it be about?"

Luis stared at him a moment, then sighed. Who was he to judge someone else's rocky relationship? He said as much for Jackson as himself, "I just hope you know what you're doing, brother."

Jackson exhaled slow, then nodded. "Keep an eye on your phone tonight. I'll text you if there are any problems."

By the time Luis turned back to Stacy, she was gone, which was probably just as well. They both had a lot to get done now in a very short amount of time.

CHAPTER EIGHT

THAT NIGHT, FOLLOWING an exhausting, frenetic afternoon getting all the final prep done in her department for the upcoming storm and bolstering outreach to the community to make sure everyone was prepared for the hurricane making landfall on the Keys later that night, Stacy and her crew were helping the Key West General maintenance guys get the final storm shutters in place over the windows in the ER waiting area.

The wind had picked up significantly since that morning, with the storm's rapid approach, and even the enormous palm trees lining the parking lot outside were starting to bend like drinking straws. Her nerves were thrumming with purpose and a pointed need to get down to the basement where Miguel was staying with one of the nurses until Stacy finished up here.

Luckily, under Luis's excellent guidance,

the hospital had been well prepared and it was only a matter of kicking their evacuation plans into high gear today. They had released as many patients as they could safely to hunker down at home, and the more critically ill or not-yet-ready-for-release patients had been moved to an emergency triage unit set up in the basement cafeteria, which had been cleared and prepped as a small hospital in itself, with the corridors and other rooms down there acting as overflow space.

A loud crash sounded against the wall outside, jarring her from her thoughts as they fit the last metal storm shutter into place over the windows. It was a public trash can, the heavy kind made of cement with a steel liner. The last huge gust had picked it up and rolled it into the building like it was nothing more than an empty soda can.

"There goes the Luigi's awning," one of the other firefighters said, pointing across the street toward a local Italian restaurant. Sure enough, the huge red-and-white-striped expanse of fabric billowed through the air like a huge kite before disappearing around the corner.

Right. If that wasn't a signal to get downstairs, Stacy didn't know what was. Pulse racing, she wiped her hands on the legs of her uniform pants then hiked her thumb toward the stairwell door. "Basement. Now. I'm going to make one more sweep up here then I'll join you."

"Want me to go with you, Captain?" Jeffrey, one of the youngest members of her crew, asked.

"No. I got it. Pretty sure everyone's downstairs now. This is just a precaution." She watched them all leave then headed through the automatic doors into the trauma bay area. She'd never seen it so eerily quiet. Even in here, you could still hear the low howl of the wind outside, like an approaching banshee. The lights flickered then came back on. The hospital had generators, thank goodness, so no worries about losing power tonight. As she walked around the circular layout of the department, checking for any stragglers, she came across one last charge nurse, filling up a supply bag with syringe packs, bandages, gauze and other necessities, in case reinforcements were needed downstairs.

Stacy walked over to help, grateful for something to do other than worry. "Anyone else in the department?"

"No. I sent them all downstairs half an hour ago," the nurse said. Her name was Ethel, and Stacy knew her in passing from her EMS runs here. Ethel's eyes kept darting toward the clock on the wall, her expression pinched with concern. "Any update on the hurricane's arrival time?"

"Not that I've heard," Stacy said, shoving handfuls of alcohol swabs and Q-tips into a pocket of the supply bag the nurse was holding. "It's a little after nine now, so another couple of hours yet before the eye wall passes. The winds are bad enough now, but they'll get worse. Rain, too. With the storm surge, we're expecting lots of flooding tomorrow. Let's hope people took the warning seriously and stayed inside."

"My little girl's at home with my husband," Ethel said, blinking hard then frowning. "I tried to call them earlier, but the lines were jammed. Sent a text, too, but haven't gotten a response yet. I hope they're okay."

Stacy felt for her. She really did. She was still praying that Jackson had made Lucy see some sense and convinced her to get off that island compound of hers, but there wasn't a thing she could do about it now. Thankfully, her mother had decided to ride out the storm on the mainland in Miami, which hopefully would avoid the brunt of Mathilda's wrath. And Stacy had Miguel here with her. And Luis. Much as she didn't want to depend on him too much, he'd become a safe harbor for her these past few days, a source of silent strength that she needed tonight more than ever. She reached over and placed her hand on Ethel's shoulder. "I'm sure they're okay. Did you have an emergency plan in place?"

"Of course." Ethel looked up then, her eyes bright with tears. "I've lived in the Keys my whole life. You always have an emergency plan ready."

"Good. Then I'm sure they've followed it and are doing exactly what they need to do." Stacy helped the nurse zip up the heavy bag then took it from her to carry out into the hall. "The best thing you can do for them right now is take care of yourself. And Ethel, I promise when all this is over, I'll go check on them personally and let you know they're okay."

Ethel gave her a watery smile. "Thank you."

"What's taking so long up here?" an irritated male voice said from the other end of the hallway, followed by a string of Spanish curses.

Luis.

Stacy sent Ethel on her way down to the basement then walked over to join him near the automatic doors. "Just finishing up a final sweep of the ER to make sure everyone's out."

"They are," he said, taking the supply bag from her and slinging it over his shoulder like it weighed nothing. "I've checked the rest of the floor, and the other units have already checked in with me in the basement. It's done. All we've left to do is ride this out."

"Let's go," she said, following him through the silent waiting area, the ominous creaks and groans from the storm shutters the only noise echoing through the empty hospital now. Her natural instinct was to take over, but Luis was in charge here. And if she'd doubted that for a second, the look on his face now convinced her. He looked tough, alpha, ready and willing to do what had to be done. But within his dark eyes flickered something else, so fast she couldn't quite identify it. Based on what he'd said at the meeting earlier, though, it made her stomach clench.

People do what they want and what they think is best, no matter the danger or who they hurt in the process, even themselves...

If those hurtful words weren't directed at her, then who else were they for? She and Luis had spent a lot of time together over the last few days. She'd let him into her home, into her bed again. If she was honest, she'd even let him into her heart, but maybe that wasn't enough.

Lord knew it hadn't been enough for her father. She'd never been good enough for him. That's why he'd left. If she'd just been a better student, a better daughter, a better person, maybe he would have stayed.

No. Her skin prickled, and her spine stiffened. Now wasn't the time to go there. And Luis wasn't her father. He'd been nothing but kind and supportive of her during their time together.

But what if he goes, too?

They pushed out the stairwell door into the basement and a scene of controlled pandemonium. All the sounds that were missing upstairs were concentrated down here—the chatter of staff and patients, the beep and buzz of monitors, the clinking of instruments and the squeaking of rubber-soled shoes and wheels on the shiny linoleum floors—creating a cacophony of busyness.

As she and Luis wove through the crowded hallways heading toward the cafeteria, they passed by patient beds pushed up against the walls, nurses and doctors attending to them as best they could under the circumstances. Portable ventilators wheezed and oxygen cylinders were attached to sides of beds, along with IV bags hung from steel trolleys. One of the residents rushed up to Luis's side with an update.

"We've sectioned the floor off, Doc, as you outlined. Surgical recovery and ICU is down that corridor." The resident pointed to a hall they passed on their right. "The geriatric patients are on the other side of the cafeteria there, and pediatrics is back on the other side of the elevators."

The lights flickered again then clicked back on, steady.

"Good work," Luis told the resident then sent him on his way.

They passed Ethel in the hall, fiddling with some cables for a patient's heart monitor, and they passed the bag of supplies back over to her for handling. As Stacy followed Luis down the corridor, she couldn't shake the feeling like she was walking through a scene from a disaster movie. She'd lived in South Florida her whole life. She'd been through plenty of storms, and as a firefighter, she worked in unpleasant or strange environments a lot, but she'd never experienced anything quite like this. It felt like the monster was outside, stalking them, waiting to get in, and it was up to her and her crew and Luis and his staff to keep the monster out. It felt almost like a war. One she was determined to win.

"Where's Miguel?" she asked, needing to see her son to reassure herself he was safe.

"He's with the nurses in the pediatric unit for now. Right before I came up to get you, I checked on him, and he was playing with Dozer, happy as a clam."

They'd stopped in front of the nonfunctioning elevators and Stacy started to respond, but before she could, the lights flickered again. Except this time they went out completely, plunging the basement into darkness. A collective gasp rippled through the corridors before the sound of machines churning on cut through the tension and suddenly there was illumination again as the generators took over. The light was different now, a sort of dull amber instead of the bright white of before, but it was better than nothing.

"C'mon," Luis said, taking her hand and tugging her toward the end of the hall where the pediatric unit was. "Let's get Miguel."

For a moment, she couldn't move, couldn't breathe, the gravity of the situation rooting her in place. Then Luis was there, turning back to her, leaning closer, to whisper in her ear, "Don't worry. You've got this. We've got this. Together." He rested his forehead against hers, his dark eyes locked on hers, genuine and steady, and for once, she didn't care what people would think. She compressed her lips and inhaled deep through her nose, seeking to calm the riot of thoughts in her head. Concentrated on the feel of his palm against hers, the warmth of his breath on her cheeks, the rise and fall of his chest.

She could do this. She would do this. Now wasn't the time to doubt or fall apart.

Stacy had spent her whole life feeling like she wasn't good enough, like she had to prove herself. Constantly trying to earn the approval of a man who'd walked out on them and never looked back. Luis seemed to accept her for who she was without judgment or reserve. He seemed pretty amazing, actually, but they'd only known each other in more than a biblical sense for a few days. It wasn't possible to love someone after that short a time.

Or was it?

Her inner turmoil ratcheted higher. Give her a fire to fight, a disaster to clear, an accident scene, and she could take care of it like nobody's business. Put her own heart, her own future at risk, and she felt completely overwhelmed and incompetent.

But she couldn't fall apart now. Nope. People were depending on her. She needed to pull it together fast. Put her emotions and her personal issues aside and get moving. She had a focus here. She had a purpose. She was a captain for the Key West Fire Department, and she had a job to do.

After another deep breath, Stacy stepped back and nodded. "Let's go."

They continued on down the hall, her heart pounding in time with her footsteps on the floor. This wasn't safe. Her heart wasn't safe with Luis anywhere around her. It was all happening so fast, yet it seemed like it had been coming for five years, ever since that night on the beach.

And despite the hurricane on their doorstep, Stacy was far more scared of her feelings for Luis.

Luis still felt as confused about what was happening with Stacy as he had earlier. Usually work centered him, cleared his head and helped him focus. But not now. As they made their way toward the small private waiting room where he'd left his son with a nurse to play with his bear and a few other toys, he kept running through his time with Stacy in his head. He'd been with several women in his life, but he'd never let anyone close to him like he had Stacy.

He wanted to pull her close and hug her, assure her that everything would be all right, even if he had no clue whether it would or not. He'd been in more than enough war zones and disaster scenes on his mission trips to know nothing was a given.

Still, he felt better with her at his side. That had to mean something.

And even if he had no idea what he was doing with regard to her and Miguel, he refused to walk away. Not yet. Maybe not ever.

They reached Miguel and he left Stacy in the room with him while he went to check on the other units before grabbing a weather radio from the makeshift command center he'd set up in the cafeteria kitchen and going back to hunker down with them for the next few hours.

Without windows or doors, they had no clue what raged outside, and the cell reception was poor down here even on the best of days. Tonight, it was dismal. One lonely bar showed on his phone screen, but he kept checking anyway, worried for his brother as much for himself and his family.

The staff were taking turns checking on patients and his wasn't for a few more hours yet, so he sat in a chair against the wall and did his best not to worry. It would be fine. Because it had to be fine. He would make it fine. That's what he did. Ride in to the rescue and save the day.

It was his purpose in life, who he was. The vow he'd made to his poor deceased parents.

I'll make you proud, I promise.

Luis wasn't so sure they'd be proud of him now, as he watched Stacy and Miguel on the floor, playing with some blocks, sharing their own little private jokes, in their own little world.

Dammit. What a mess he'd made of this.

Maybe he was wrong to try to insert himself into their lives the way he was. Stacy had told him she'd been fine, happy, before he'd returned. Was that the reason she seemed to be shutting him out now? Did they truly not need him? Were they better off without him?

He loved his son more than his own life, would do anything for the boy. Even walk out of his life again if that was truly the best thing for him.

And Stacy… Well, she'd rocked his world, in more ways than one.

He'd never imagined on that long-ago

night on that moonlit beach that she'd be so perfect for him in all the ways that mattered. Not just sexually, either. She was smart and funny and sweet and strong. She was everything he wanted in a mate.

Except emotionally available.

Every time he thought about her father leaving her behind, making her feel less than, he wanted to hit something. Mainly the man who'd turned his back on his family. He'd lost his own parents during a treacherous crossing of the Florida Straits, but that had been different. His parents had loved him so much that they'd given up their lives to try to give him a better future. Her father had turned his back on Stacy and her mother, forcing them into a life of struggle and poverty.

Hands fisted, Luis clenched his teeth, a muscle ticking near his tense jaw.

Luis wanted to make up for that loss, wanted to show Stacy that she was good enough, that she was enough. Period. Amen. But each time he got closer, she shut him out.

"Mommy, why are we down here?" Miguel asked, cutting through Luis's turbulent thoughts.

"Because it's storming outside, honey," she said, handing him another block. "We need to stay down here to be safe until it's over."

"Where's Grandma?" the boy asked.

"She's in Miami with her friend." At her son's concerned look, she smoothed his hair with her fingers. "Grandma will be fine. I talked to her earlier today and she'll be back with us just as soon as she can be, I promise."

Miguel gave a small nod, frowning. "Daddy's here."

"Yes, he is." Stacy glanced his way, holding his gaze a moment before looking away again, her deep blue eyes unreadable.

Luis wanted to shout that he'd always be there, come hell or high water or anything Mother Nature might throw their way. He'd be there for as long as they'd have him, but given Stacy's reaction to his proclamations earlier, he didn't think that was wise. So, instead, he got up to pace away some of the pent-up energy inside him threatening to burst out of his skin. Finally, he couldn't take it anymore. Feeling claustrophobic and conflicted, he headed for the door. "Stay here with him. I'm going to see if they need help out there."

Thankfully, they did. As he'd predicted, several new injuries had arrived along with the storm's gales. The EMTs had been directed to bring any patients that weren't hunkered down to the basement, and now there were several. Mainly people who'd waited until the last minute to board up and had gotten caught in the storm and lashed by flying debris.

He treated a man with a nasty gash on his forehead and a woman with a broken wrist from a fall, then headed to the crisis triage center in the cafeteria kitchen to help field radio calls. Other members of the Emergency Response Team were there also, including members of the police and fire departments.

He'd done work like this on several of his previous mission trips, so it came as second nature to him. There were already plenty of reports that had come in as the first bands lashed the Keys, mainly building damage. No casualty reports yet, though, thank goodness. He dealt with a call from a home health agency about several elderly clients they hadn't had time to check on before Mathilda hit but reassured the caller that most likely they were safe. If they'd been living down here for any length of time, they'd know about hurricanes. Just in case, though, he passed those notes on to law enforcement so they could add the residents to their list of people to check on once the storm had passed.

Meanwhile, the weather radios crackled on in the background with reports of black skies and hammering winds. Cars were being flipped and roofs were being peeled off like tin cans. Scary stuff indeed.

Luis pulled out his phone to check for a message from Jackson. His brother had told him he'd text him tonight to let him know he'd made it safely to Lucy's place. Based on the intel now, if he'd gotten there, Jackson would likely be stuck out on Big Pine Key for the duration of the storm. No way could anyone drive on the Overseas Highway in this. He prayed Jackson wouldn't try something reckless like he usually did. His brother was one of the bravest men Luis had ever known. One of the best, too. But he let his heart rule too often over his head.

Not something Luis had ever been accused of. Until now.

The buzzing of his phone in his hand made Luis jump.

He looked down to see a short text shining on his screen.

At Big Pine Key. Won't make it back.

Luis was happy his brother was safe. Less so that he would have to continue to be interim incident commander. He knew how much that position had meant to Jackson and how hard it must've been for him to give it up, even temporarily. Lucy must be very special to his brother indeed.

There was no time to dwell on that, however, as the storm raged on, radio calls continued to come in and there were patients to treat and a community to keep together during a hurricane.

After an hour or so, Luis needed a break and turned his position over to another team member who was fresh off break. He wandered back down the corridors, checking patients as he went. According to his smart watch, it was close to eleven now and things had quieted a bit in the basement even as conditions worsened outside. He passed by a gurney where a man with a cut on his arm was telling the nurse who was treating him about what he'd seen on his way into the ER.

"Rain coming down in sheets. You couldn't see two feet in front of you," the guy said, eyes wide. "Stuff flying through the air, smashing into windows. I've been down here through three hurricanes, but ain't never seen anything like this one. She's a doozy!"

Finally, he turned the corner and headed back down the hall toward the room where Stacy and Miguel were. He took a deep breath. The angsty knot in his stomach that had been there all day was still present, he'd just learned to ignore it. His back and neck ached and the thought of lying down for a bit to rest his eyes, especially with Stacy, sounded wonderful.

He stopped by a vending machine and bought them some waters and snacks then opened the door to the room with his elbow and went in. Stacy was sitting against the wall in the chair he'd vacated earlier, and she motioned for him to be quiet before pointing down at a sleeping Miguel on the floor. She'd managed to find some extra blankets and pillows, it looked like, and had made a bed for their son in one corner of the small room. In the opposite corner sat a stack of linens for them to use.

There was only one lamp in the room and the bulb looked like it was on its last legs, given the weak light it was putting out. Still, it was better than nothing, so he took a seat in the other chair beside Stacy and handed her a water and bag of chips. "The best I could do for dinner."

She laughed and took her food. "Thanks. I got Miguel something from the vending machines, too, before he fell asleep. Poor guy."

"How's he holding up?" Luis asked around a mouthful of pretzels. "He seemed okay earlier."

"He's good. A bit agitated, but I think sleep will help with that. Usually does." She glanced at him. "How are things out there?"

"Hectic." He filled her in on everything he'd seen and heard while they ate, including the text from Jackson. "If he's there with Lucy, she'll be fine. My brother was in the coast guard and there's no one I'd want at my back in a dangerous situation more than Jackson. They'll be okay."

"I hope so." She finished her chips then tossed their bags into the trash. "Lucy's special."

"Hmm. She seemed very intent on her job when I met her at the last ERT meeting. You two are good friends?"

"We are. I met her after she moved here last year. She's going to help me get a service dog for Miguel."

"Oh. That's wonderful." He stretched then winced as his right shoulder ached from sitting in one position too long taking those radio calls. "Ouch."

"Stiff?" Stacy asked walking back over to sit beside him again.

"A little. Nothing I can't handle."

Stacy smiled. "Well, Jackson picked the right man to be interim IC."

"Thanks. Though there isn't much for me to do. My brother had it all set up before he left." He shifted slightly to look at her. "And you did a fine job with the fire department, getting everything done today on such short notice."

"Thanks," she said, though her tone sounded a bit flat.

Curious, he shifted slightly to face her better. "What?"

"Nothing."

"Stacy?" he prodded. Maybe it wasn't a good thing to do with the stress between them, but they were trapped here with each other for hours. Why not put it to good use talking some of this out? "Tell me."

At first, he thought she'd shut him out again, but then she sighed and rested her head back against the wall. "I know I'm good at my job. I wouldn't be a captain if I wasn't. But I always wonder if I'm good enough. Not as a firefighter, but as a person."

The urge to punch her errant father returned full force, and Luis shoved his hands in the pockets of his lab coat so she couldn't see his fists. The rawness in her voice, the intensity in those words, made his heart pinch for her. "You're a good person, Stacy."

She blinked, the dim light in the room catching the moisture in her eyes, and his breath caught. He forced himself to relax and took her hand. "I mean it. You're a wonderful woman. An excellent firefighter. And the best mom ever to Miguel. I don't think a person could ask for anything more."

"You only see the good in me." Stacy smiled and leaned closer to rest her head on his shoulder.

This close, the sweet floral scent of her shampoo surrounded him, the warmth of her cheek pressed against the side of his throat. The need to touch her, to hold her, to make her see all the incredible things he did when he saw her, jolted through him like electricity. But still he held back, conscious of their son sleeping a short distance away and wary of ruining this moment between them.

"True," he whispered at last. "But man, is it glorious."

Stacy raised her head then to look at him, her beautiful blue eyes and long eyelashes highlighted by the dim glow of the lamp. Even though they were still in the busy basement of the hospital, this felt so private, and he was grateful for their tiny spot to be alone.

She reached up and traced his profile with her finger, then smiled, banishing his shadows. "Thank you."

He kissed the tip of her finger then settled back, closing his eyes as he gathered her closer into his side. Luckily these chairs were padded and had no arms, which made for better snuggling. At first Stacy didn't move. Then she wrapped her arms around his middle, like a hug. It felt good. It felt right.

He'd spent the last few years always working, always running, always trying to be whatever he thought he needed to be to fulfill his vow to his deceased birth parents. And none of that had included letting anyone close to his heart. So now, sitting here, with Stacy, the sensations sizzling through him almost hurt. Still, Stacy didn't let go. And finally, after what felt like a small eternity, the tension knotted inside him drained away. The same thing had happened their first night together years ago, he realized, but at the time, he'd put it down to the alcohol and the passion of the moment.

Now, though, he knew it to be something

more. Something real. Something bigger than he'd ever experienced before, and he was scared. His chest ached. Not from exertion, but from emotion. Yearning, need, desire, affection. All of them swirled into a riotous blend of color and sound and sensation.

Impossible as it seemed to his logical mind, his one-night stand had actually brought the perfect woman for him into his life. He hadn't seen it at the time, and he was still trying to understand it.

He traced the backs of his fingers down her cheeks, pulling back from her embrace just enough to tilt her chin up and kiss her. He was hesitant at first, not wanting to push where he wasn't wanted, but then he deepened the kiss as her hand slid into his hair and she responded beneath him. Just as she started to move across his lap to straddle him, Miguel murmured in his sleep behind them, and they both froze.

This time, it was Stacy who rested her forehead against his and smiled. "Guess we should stop."

Luis laughed. "Guess we should."

Stacy climbed off him just as something bumped into the other side of the door. Luis straightened and raked a hand through his hair. He needed a shave and probably a shower as well, but both of those would have to wait.

"I should go see what's going on," he said, getting up. "You okay here with Miguel?"

"Yep," she said, yawning. "I'll probably take a nap myself before my next shift."

"Good idea." He opened the door then looked back at her. "Sleep well. See you later."

"See you."

Luis closed the door and headed back toward the cafeteria command center, unable to wipe the silly smile from his face, even as the storm raged around them.

CHAPTER NINE

STACY DID SLEEP, more exhausted than she thought after the day's craziness, and when she woke it took her a moment to realize where she was. Through the dim light of the room, she spotted Miguel still asleep across from her, his thumb in his mouth and his bear, Dozer, tucked at his side beneath his cast.

She went to shift slightly from where she was lying on the floor, having pushed the chairs back to the corner to make room to stretch out, and found a warm, heavy weight draped over her waist, pinning her in place. Next came the awareness of the solid warm body pressed behind hers.

Slowly, she turned her head slightly to see Luis asleep behind her, his handsome features relaxed and so open it made her heart ache. He'd called her a good person.

He treated her as an equal. He seemed too good to be true.

But is he?

Her hip hurt from staying in one spot too long, and eventually, she had to move. She sat up carefully, trying to avoid waking the two guys in her life, and failed when Miguel stirred then awoke with a start.

"Mommy?" he wailed, reaching for her, his little face scrunched. "I had a bad dream!"

She rushed to him and held him close as Luis jolted up, rumpled and groggy and far too gorgeous than a man had a right to be. Stacy bit back a grin at his obvious disorientation and hugged her son closer, kissing the top of his dark little head. "It's okay, honey. It was just a dream. You're okay."

"What happened?" Luis asked, squinting over at her. "What time is it?"

"It's..." She checked her watch. "About 2:00 a.m., and your son had a nightmare."

Following another kiss and a squeeze, she set Miguel away from her and scooted back. He seemed fine now, as he did after most of his bad dreams, forgetting them promptly as new adventures took hold. The little boy climbed out from beneath his covers and itched his arm above his cast.

"I need to potty, Mommy," Miguel said, rubbing his eyes with his free hand.

"Me, too," Stacy said, climbing to her feet as well. "And then we need to eat before Mommy needs to work for a bit."

Luis yawned and stood as well. "The cafeteria is serving cold meals for staff and patients. How about we all freshen up then meet again in the hallway?"

"Sounds good." Stacy got her son squared away and then herself while Luis headed to the staff locker rooms for a quick shower and shave. By the time they met up again, he looked fresh and alert while she still felt a bit musty without her coffee.

They went into the cafeteria and stood in line with other members of the staff to get food. Everyone was looking a little worse for wear as the hurricane continued to rage on outside. From here, they were a bit insulated from the chaos, but from the conversations she heard around her, things were pretty bad outside. Power was out for most of the Keys, and they were saying it could be days before it was restored. The local emergency shelters that had been set up were close to capacity as well, and the worst of the flooding was yet to come.

She picked up Miguel and held him in her

arms as they moved closer in the food line. The room was noisy and Miguel tucked his head against her neck, not liking the clamor of voices all trying to talk over one another. Luis pushed two trays, one for himself and one for her and Miguel, stocking them each with water and food as they made their way through the line. Finally, they found seats at the end of a crowded table of cops and firefighters and Stacy sat Miguel on her lap as she handed him a fork to eat with.

One of the guys from her crew, Harley, was sitting down the bench from her, so while her son ate, Stacy asked him for a rundown on the conditions outside.

"The eye wall's passing over now," Harley said. "It's weird. The rain's stopped and you can see the stars. It'll pick up again soon, though, Captain."

No doubt about that. The winds were usually strongest around the eye wall, too, so they were far from out of danger yet. Luis stayed silent eating his food like he feared someone would take it away from him. Miguel did the same. One more similarity between father and son. She smiled again. Luis had shaved, too, she noticed. His still-damp hair shined beneath the amber emergency lights overhead.

"I'll have one of the nurses watch Miguel for me while I check in with my crew and see what needs to be done next," Stacy said. "What about you?"

"I've got some patients to check on and some other logistics to handle."

"Any more texts from Jackson?" she asked, thinking again of her friend Lucy.

"No, not yet." Luis frowned and pushed away his empty cereal bowl. "But since the storm is heading north, they're probably still getting the brunt of it. Hopefully, we'll all be in the clear by morning and they can get out and assess the damage."

They finished their meal in silence, the voices dying down around them to a dull roar.

Miguel wanted down, and she let him slip off her lap with a warning not to go far. Luis tracked their son's movement, his expression unreadable. She'd never felt such a deep, instant connection to someone like she did to Luis, and it was unsettling. It didn't matter that they'd only known each other—really known each other—for such a short time. It was what it was. And what it was, was exhilarating. Exhilarating and excruciating and enormously terrifying, all rolled into one.

Luis transferred his gaze from their son to her, and the look in his dark eyes made the hairs on the back of her neck stand at attention. "Are we friends, Stacy?"

"Uh…" She frowned, not sure how to categorize what they were to each other at that point. "I don't know. Why?"

He reached over and took her hand, gaze steady on hers. "What if I want to be more?"

Stunned, she sat there blinking at him. Seriously? He was going to do this here? "Uh…"

That seemed the only word she was capable of at the moment.

Lacing his fingers with hers, Luis continued. "I realize my timing isn't the best here, but I need to say this. Stacy, I—"

"Dr. Durand?" a nurse called over the din in the room. "We need you right away, please!"

Stacy cursed internally. Seemed fate was forever interfering in their story. Luis scrubbed a hand over his face and flashed an apologetic smile. "Duty calls."

"Apparently." She raised an annoyed brow at him then stood to throw away their trash and open up the seats for someone else. "Go on. I'll get Miguel and get him to his nurse babysitter. I'll see you later after my shift."

She watched him walk away, feeling like they'd lost something precious in that moment.

The next few hours passed in a blur of cases and damage reports and orders for rescue teams to deploy to different areas of Key West as Hurricane Mathilda slowly made her way northward, leaving behind a path of destruction for the Emergency Response Team to clean up.

For his part, Luis was glad for the distraction. A strange restlessness buzzed inside him following their interrupted conversation this morning, and he felt like he had to keep moving, keep pushing forward or something bad would happen.

Up until Stacy had reappeared in his life, he'd felt safe and secure on his path. It had always served him well, putting the needs of others before his own. But now, he saw a future he wanted for himself, the rest of the world's thoughts and concerns about it be damned. A future with Stacy and Miguel by his side, and all he had to do was reach for it. Well, reach for it and convince her that it would work and that he wasn't going anywhere.

He couldn't say exactly when the switch

had flipped for him from coparent to friend to lover to…*more*. But flip it had, and now the deep sense of yearning in his chest, the near-constant ache for more that had dogged him since the loss of his parents way back when had transformed into certainty. Over the past few days, spending time with Stacy, getting to know her, and their son through her, had changed his feelings from like to love. And it wasn't just physical, either, though that was definitely there. No. He loved her heart, and her intelligence. Her drive and her desire to help others. Even her stubbornness was sexy as hell, when it wasn't directed at him, of course.

With Stacy, he'd found what he was looking for. An equal. A partner. A soul mate.

He'd spotted her a few times throughout the predawn hours, meeting with her crew and coordinating rescue efforts with the local ambulance authority. She was impressive, no doubt about it, and it made him love her even more. There was nothing sexier than competence for him, and his Stacy had that in spades.

She was excellent at her job and an excellent mother and would make an excellent wife, too, one day, he had no doubt, if and when they got to that point. Together, they'd save the world and raise their son.

Now he just needed to convince her of that, too.

By late morning, the storm had passed completely and they'd gotten the first floor opened up again. He went outside with the cops to assess the damage and was pleased to see that the hospital hadn't fared too badly overall. There were some broken windows and lots of downed trees and power lines, but the generators were holding up well and now that conditions were improving, weatherwise, restoration crews could start moving in to get life back to normal again. Jackson's early planning had meant that all of it was running smoothly. Luis was sure his brother would get the promotion he'd worked so hard for, even if he'd temporarily turned over command to Luis.

And speaking of Jackson, shortly after noon Luis finally spoke to his brother. Cell service was still spotty but getting better.

"How did you fare on Big Pine Key?" Luis asked as he stood outside the hospital, glad for some fresh air after hours locked down in the basement.

"It's been..." Jackson hesitated, then sighed. "It's been interesting. We're okay up here. Lucy's house took on quite a bit of damage, though, and from what I can see there's a lot of cleanup to do around here. The highway's completely blocked, so I'm not sure when I'll get back. How about Key West?"

"About the same, brother." He told Jackson about the wind damage and the reports of several cars off the road and a couple of older residents trapped in their homes by floodwaters. "I'll let the flight crew know about your situation and see if they can send someone down to pick you up today. Any casualties?"

"No. I got attacked by a gator when I first arrived, but that's about it."

"I'm sorry?" Luis scowled. "You what?"

Jackson laughed. "Long story. I'll tell you about it later. I'm glad to hear things are going well down there. I should get back to Lucy. My battery's about dead anyway. Take care, brother."

"You, too," Luis said. "I'll send that helicopter soon."

The call ended, and Luis headed back inside. A glance at his smart watch showed that Stacy's shift was almost done, and a fresh wave of doctors and staff were slowly making their way in to relieve those who'd been on duty all night, including Luis. Signs of recovery and goodwill were popping up all around them, including several people who'd set up grills around the parking lot and were cooking food for staff and anyone else who needed a hot meal after the storm.

He wanted to stand under a hot shower for days, then fall into bed and sleep for a few more. But first, he had something else to do and a newly formed plan in his mind of how to go about it.

CHAPTER TEN

STACY HAD JUST finished up dispatching her last crew to an accident on the edge of town when she turned to find Luis in the doorway of the cafeteria kitchen, smiling at her. He'd changed out of his scrubs and lab coat and had on the jeans and T-shirt he'd left her apartment in the day before.

"You look beat," he said.

"I feel beat." She stretched then rubbed her sore neck. "Have you been outside yet?"

"I have." He moved into the room to stand before her. "It's messy, but not horrible. The cleanup is already underway. Why don't you go clean up in the staff locker room? I checked on Miguel and he's doing fine with the nurse, and I even found you a spare set of scrubs to change into when you're done. Meet me back here. I've got a surprise for you."

She was a bit taken aback but in no fit

state to argue. For once, Stacy was too tired anyway, so she did as he asked, taking a shower and brushing her teeth using one of the disposable kits in the locker room. She changed into the pink scrubs he'd set on the bench in the locker room for her, then stared down at her black work boots. They'd look pretty silly with the scrubs, but they were all she had here with her. She hadn't thought to bring a change of clothes from her apartment, what with everything else on her mind.

Once that was done, she grabbed her phone from the charger in the locker room and checked in with her mother via text. She was doing fine in Miami, though the storm was still a bit stronger there. No word from Lucy yet, but if anything had happened to her and Jackson, Stacy was sure Luis would've mentioned it.

Finally, she checked her appearance in the mirror. She'd smoothed her wet hair back into a low ponytail at the base of her neck and scrubbed her face clean. Her cheeks were pink, but she wished she'd had some makeup to put on.

Oh, well. Nothing for it now. Besides, considering what they'd been through last night, makeup should be the least of her concerns. She headed out of the locker room and back to the cafeteria to find Luis waiting for her in the hall. In his hand was a tray covered with aluminum foil. Even from where she stood, the smell of barbecue wafted around her, and her stomach growled. In his other hand was a bag she hoped held utensils to eat the food.

"Where did you get that?" she asked, walking up to him.

"It's a surprise." He winked then checked out her outfit. "Nice look."

She nudged him with her shoulder and chuckled. "Are you sure Miguel's okay?"

"Yep." Luis pushed open the stairwell door with his shoulder then held it for her. "When I looked in on him right before you got here, he had a stack of books and a willing nurse to help him read them. Our son's in heaven."

"Sounds like it." Stacy took the bag from him and headed upstairs, Luis behind her. "So where are we going?"

"I thought we'd get out of here for a bit. When I was out earlier, I took a glance at the beach nearby. Looks safe enough."

"Sounds good." They pushed out into the lobby, and she squinted into the hazy sunlight streaming in through the windows. They'd started removing some of the storm shutters, and she got her first look at the damage. Shards of glass sparkled on the tiled floor from some of the shattered windows, along with palm fronds and assorted trash. Outside, the air still felt humid on her skin, but the oppressive heat of earlier was gone. In its wake a steady breeze blew, nothing like the onslaught of the night before. People were out wandering around, snapping pictures or gawking over missing roofs and caved-in buildings. Overall, it wasn't as bad as she'd expected, though this was only a small part of their community. There'd been other places, closer to the water, where the damage had been much worse, she knew from her crews out and about in the city.

Luis took her hand and led her across the empty street and down the path to the beach. There were more palm fronds down here and scattered debris, but they managed to find a clear spot to sit.

"There's a towel in the bag for us to sit on," he said.

She pulled it out and spread it on the wet, firm sand. The ocean was quiet now, dark and steady. They settled down and Luis pulled the foil off the tray to reveal a platter of barbecued meats, most likely from one of the vendors she'd spotted in the parking lot on their way here. It was so thoughtful, it made Stacy's chest squeeze. "Thank you."

"My pleasure," Luis said, shrugging like it wasn't a big deal. He dug in the bag again and came out with two paper plates and plastic flatware. Then he pulled out two bottled waters and handed her one. "Nothing fancy, but we both deserve a good meal after last night."

"Agreed."

They dug into the food like starving people, chatting around mouthfuls, just enjoying the fresh air and freedom after hours in captivity.

"So," Stacy said at last, full and sated. She gave Luis a side glance, still uncertain where things stood with him after their interrupted conversation earlier that day. When she'd thought he'd been about to suggest they take things to the next level, she'd been frozen. There was no other way to describe it. She liked Luis. Loved him, even. But were they ready for a committed relationship?

She'd seen how that had turned out for her parents, and she never wanted Miguel to go through something like that. Not that Luis was anything like her father, but still. She wasn't ready. They weren't ready.

Were they?

Luis wrapped up their trash in the tinfoil then leaned back on one elbow, watching her. "So."

He turned to stare out at the ocean, giving her a glimpse of his perfect profile, his dark hair ruffled by the breeze, the scents of sand and sea around them. From somewhere above a plaintive seagull cried, and she got the uneasy feeling that this was an important moment, though she wasn't sure why.

Finally, Luis looked over at her and said, "I think we should try to make this work between us. As a couple. For Miguel's sake."

Blood rushed in her ears, and she forced herself to breathe. "Isn't that what we're doing?"

"I mean more formally." Luis sat up and reached for her hand, and Stacy pulled away before she could stop herself. The hurt look on his face nearly gutted her. He bit his lip and stared down at the towel for a moment before saying, "I don't mean marriage. Neither of us is ready for that yet, I don't think."

The air in her lungs whooshed out in a great, relieved rush before she could stop it. "Oh, thank God."

At his startled look, she amended, "I just mean… Well…"

"I know what you meant." He shook his

head and gave a small, sad snort. "I just don't want to go backward from where we are now, Stacy. Do you understand?"

She took that in a minute then nodded. "I think I do."

"Good." Luis reached for her hand again, and this time she let him take it. The slow skim of his thumb over her knuckles was hypnotic. "What happens next then, Stacy?"

She licked her lips, not sure exactly what he wanted her to say, so she went with the truth. "I'm not sure. The last few days have been…odd."

"Odd?"

"Yes." She shrugged. "I mean, challenging. Maybe that's a better word. In a lot of ways. With work and life, and…us."

"Agreed." He exhaled slowly. "I didn't expect to feel so close to you and Miguel so quickly."

"But you do?"

"*Si.* I do." He kissed her fingers, his dark eyes warm. "I feel like I've known you my whole life. Like when I'm with you, I'm home."

Her breath caught and her chest squeezed, and if she hadn't been sitting down, she feared she might have melted into a puddle of goo at his feet at the sweetness of that.

And she wasn't the melting-goo sort of girl usually. But Luis brought that out in her. That was what was so great about him. And what was so scary.

Stacy turned slightly to face him and slid her arms around his neck, tipping her head to the side. "I'm comfortable with you, too. But this is very new to me. After what I told you about my father and my past, you know it's hard for me to let people in, to depend on other people. But I'm willing to try, with you."

"That's all I can ask," he said, leaning in to close the gap between them and kiss her.

The ease with which they seemed to fall into a comfortable routine over the next seven days lulled Luis into a sense of security he'd never expected to find. There was much work to be done, both at the hospital and out on the streets of Key West, and between himself and Stacy, they were pulling extra shifts right and left just to cover it all.

There'd been an influx of patients to the ER following the storm, everything from minor scrapes and bruises to more serious broken bones and concussions from falling debris, and even one poor guy who'd required a partial amputation of his leg due to an infection that had set in after wading through polluted floodwater to rescue his neighbors. Still, it felt good to be busy and useful, and Luis was in his element. He'd even gone down to one of the emergency shelters near Key West General on his breaks several times to help them feed the hungry and displaced. It helped satisfy his niggling conscience, the tiny voice whispering in his head that he wasn't doing enough to be of service, that he should be traveling more, that there were other, harder-hit places that were much worse off than the Keys and much poorer to boot.

He managed to shove that voice aside, knowing he was where he needed to be right now.

Personally, things were moving along at a good clip, too. He'd been spending pretty much every night at Stacy's, giving them even more privacy to explore their relationship and figure out what the next step should be. After their talk on the beach, they'd begun taking turns watching Miguel while the other one worked. Luckily, their shifts weren't on the same schedule, so when one was away, the other was available. Miguel loved spending more time with his daddy and was getting to the point where he refused to go to sleep until both Mommy and Daddy had read him a story.

Luis had even taken Stacy and Miguel to his house for dinner one night. He'd been so proud to show them around the place and let them see what his hard work and dedication had allowed him to build. Miguel loved all the windows overlooking the gardens outside and the pool, too. Plus, there was a large room upstairs Luis planned to turn into a playroom for his son and fill with toys and books, just as soon as he had the free time to do it. Stacy had clearly been impressed, too, if a bit quieter about it. At first, Luis had been concerned that she didn't like it, but she'd assured him that wasn't it at all. She was just awed by it all, she said.

One day, he hoped to move them both in there and become a real family. There was even a separate guest house where her mother could stay when she visited.

Jackson had made it back fine from Big Pine Key, too. His leg was healing nicely, though he'd yet to fully explain to Luis what had happened. His brother was cranky as all get-out, too, moody and miserable, though they'd had precious little time to talk, what with Jackson overseeing the disaster relief and Luis busy with Miguel and Stacy. Someday soon, though, they needed to sit down and hash it all out, if for no other reason than to try to lift Jackson out of his surly mood.

Speaking of icy exteriors, he scrolled through his tablet to bring up the chart on the new patient in trauma bay two before knocking on the door and walking in to introduce himself.

"Hello, I'm Dr. Luis Durand. What seems to be the problem today?" he asked, professional smile firmly in place. He glanced down at his tablet again. "Mr. Rojas."

"My chest hurts," the older man said. According to his file he was seventy-one. "Thought I should have it checked out."

"Good thinking." Luis set his tablet aside to check the man's vitals. "I've looked over your chart, and there's no family history of heart disease."

"No, sir," the man said, wincing slightly when Luis pressed his stethoscope to his chest below his sternum. "Ow."

"That hurts?" Luis frowned. "Any injury to the area? Were you struck by anything there, or walk into anything?"

"Not that I can recall. It was fine this morning." Mr. Rojas took a deep breath when Luis prompted him to. He seemed a bit groggy, and his blood pressure was a tad low, but nothing too far out of the ideal range. "I was on my way to the gas station to fill up for the generator when the pain started. It scared me, so I came right over here. But I need to let my wife know where I am so she won't worry."

"We'll take care of letting your wife know, Mr. Rojas." Luis straightened and went over to check the EKG results that the nurse had running. All normal. Blood work, too.

"Right." Luis picked up his tablet and entered his orders. "I'm going to get an X-ray so I can see what's happening inside there, since everything seems normal so far. We can do that right down here, so it shouldn't take long." He went to the door to wave the nurse in. "I'll be back once I've seen those results."

Fifteen minutes later, Luis stood staring at the images on the computer screen at the nurses' station. At first glance, it all seemed normal, but then Luis squinted and leaned in farther. The aorta seemed wider than it should have been, which was concerning. The placement of the suspected enlargement coincided with where Mr. Rojas was experiencing his pain, too. He sat down and searched the hospital's records to see if the man had been treated at Key West General before and had any previous chest X-rays done. Sure enough, there was one from two years prior, when he'd been treated for flu and possible pneumonia. Pulling those films up onscreen, Luis compared them side by side and discovered that, yes, there was definitely enlargement there. Enough to make Luis suspect a possible rupture. It would explain all Mr. Rojas's symptoms and would require immediate surgery to repair. He contacted the cardiothoracic surgeon on call and explained the case to him before heading back in the patient's room.

The nurse was there, checking the monitors. "I called his wife. She's on her way."

"Good." Luis took a seat on the wheeled stool in the corner and moved to the patient's bedside. "Mr. Rojas, I've got good news and bad news for you. Which would you like first?"

The man grimaced. "Give me the bad. Considering what we've been through the last couple weeks, I want to get it over with."

"Okay. I looked at your X-ray results and compared them with the films you had done here at the hospital a few years ago, and it appears that you've ruptured your aorta."

"My what?"

"Aorta. It's the major blood vessel that

runs from your heart through your torso."
He pulled up a diagram on his tablet to show
the man, pointing to the spot where the trouble was.

"How did that happen?" Mr. Rojas frowned.
"I haven't done anything to that area, like I
said. And I've been working to clean up the
damage around my property, but nothing too
strenuous."

"It's hard to say." Luis lowered the tablet to his lap again. "Most likely there was
a congenital weakness in that area that has
been present from birth. Without this rupture, we might never have known it was
there. Now that it's burst, however, we need
to get it fixed. And fast, so you don't lose
too much blood."

"Fixed?" Mr. Rojas's eyes widened. "You
mean surgery?"

"Yes. I've contacted the specialist, and
he's on his way to consult. He'll be able to
give you more information about the procedure, but it's a good thing you came in today.
It probably saved your life."

Ms. Rojas arrived a short time later, followed
by the cardiothoracic surgeon, who took over
the case from Luis with a hearty thank-you.

"Good work, Dr. Durand," the surgeon

said. "Spotting a rupture like that on films is difficult. Lots of doctors miss it."

"I've had lots of practice discerning issues in less-than-optimal conditions," Luis said, stepping aside as the staff wheeled Mr. Rojas, with his wife by his side, out of the trauma bay and into the elevator to whisk him up to the OR. "Good luck with the surgery."

After that, things slowed down a bit, and Luis took the opportunity to catch up on all the paperwork he'd put off since before the hurricane. He had a small office on the first floor, near the ER, and he holed himself up in there with his stacks of paper to get some of it off his desk.

Unfortunately, he only got about an hour in before his phone buzzed in his pocket, interrupting his workflow. Luis pulled it out and answered without checking the caller ID. "Dr. Durand."

"Luis?" a voice said through the line. One he hadn't heard in over a year.

"Xavier." Luis dropped his pen on the desk and sat back, smiling. "How are you? Where are you?"

"I'm good. Busy as hell, but good. We just arrived in Honduras. They got hit hard by a storm down here, too, you know."

He did know. Luis had kept an eye on the news reports out of Central America more out of habit than anything. Docs on Duty, the charity group he had been a part of for his mission trips, spent a lot of time in that area helping the poor and underprivileged get the supplies and medical care they needed. He'd been eyeing the tropical storm that had formed right on Mathilda's heels and had cringed to hear that it had not only strengthened into a hurricane itself, but one even stronger than Mathilda had been. The people of Honduras and the surrounding countries hadn't stood a chance.

"How bad is it?" Luis asked, scrubbing a hand over his face. He'd gone to Haiti after Hurricane Matthew, a category five storm, and had seen the devastation firsthand—two hundred thousand homes destroyed, over five hundred people dead, $2.8 billion of destruction. The small island nation was still recovering. It was times like that his near-eidetic memory was more curse than blessing. For years, each time he closed his eyes, he'd see the faces of the survivors, hear their cries for help, feel the anguish of those who'd lost everything. The memories from that time replayed over and over his head, spurring him onward to do more, be of more service. Even now, he felt the pull to rush to action, despite all the things tethering him to his new life in Key West.

"Worse than you can imagine. The damage from the storm was bad enough, but now we've got landslides on top of it." Xavier took a deep breath then said the thing Luis had been dreading since he'd answered the call. "Look, buddy. I know you left this behind and you've settled down in Florida, but we could really use your help here."

The tug on Luis's soul was strong, almost as strong as the one keeping him here for Stacy and Miguel. He bit his lip and sighed. "I can't. I'm head of emergency medicine at Key West General now. I've got commitments and constraints." He tapped his fingers on the desk to expel some of the adrenaline burning through his bloodstream. He couldn't walk away from his life here, not now. His community needed him. Stacy needed him. Miguel needed him. "Sorry, but I just can't. Perhaps I can pass the word around to my colleagues, though, see if anyone else is interested."

"Thanks. I appreciate it, but we need people with experience in these conditions." Xavier murmured something to someone off the line then got back on with Luis. "Listen, we'd work with you on the logistics and the scheduling. I know you've got other stuff going on right now and I wouldn't ask if I wasn't desperate, but we really need help here, Luis. Please at least think about it. One last time? Even if it's only for a month or a few weeks."

One last time.

After the call ended, Luis sat there at his desk, staring down at his paperwork without really seeing it, torn and twisted inside. When he'd left the charity the previous year, it was with the assurance that they had more than enough adequate doctors to take over his position with the team. But the past twelve months had been beyond rough on a global scale, and it seemed their resources had been depleted faster than the charity could recoup them. If the call had come six months earlier—hell, even last month—he'd have put in for an extended leave and gone without a second thought, but now…

Well, now he had more than himself to consider. He had Stacy and Miguel. He'd made a commitment to them, too. Had promised to be there for them and try to work things out. And given Stacy's past, she would not take his leaving again well, no matter the reason.

He felt stuck between a rock and a hard place with no easy solution. He needed to talk to Stacy. Thankfully they were both off tonight, for once. He'd planned to have a romantic evening at his house. Cook dinner, relax, let Miguel play with his toys while he and Stacy enjoyed each other's company.

Tension knotted tight within him. The call to service was one he felt obligated to answer, but Stacy needed him now, too. They were just starting out on this new path together and he didn't want to do anything to risk their relationship or the one with his son by leaving again. And given Stacy's past, there was the possibility she'd see it as a betrayal. But he wanted things to be open and honest between them, so he'd tell her. They'd discuss it and then they'd decide. Maybe it wouldn't be as bad as he imagined.

The dread knotting in his gut said otherwise.

CHAPTER ELEVEN

"LISTEN, SWEETHEART," STACY'S mother said over the phone line as Stacy finished up in her office at the fire station. "I'm thinking of staying up here in Miami awhile longer, if that's all right with you."

"You're an adult, Mom. You don't need my permission." Stacy switched her cell phone to her other ear as she tidied her desk. "Is everything okay with your friend?"

"Oh yes. He's doing much better now. In fact, we're thinking about taking a short trip to Bermuda to celebrate his recovery, once they get all this storm damage resolved."

"Oh." Stacy paused for a second. Maybe this thing between her mom and her mom's new friend went beyond platonic. If so, it would be the first time in Stacy's memory. She hoped for her mother's sake it was good. Her mom deserved it. She'd worked so hard raising Stacy on her own. She deserved love and happiness. She just wished she'd gotten to meet the mysterious man first. Concerned on her mother's behalf, she said, "What's his name again?"

"Ted, dear," her mother chided. "And you knew that."

Stacy couldn't help grinning. She'd been doing that a lot lately since Luis had reappeared in her life. "You're right, I did. Well, that's fine. I'll need to shuffle Miguel's schedule, but it shouldn't be too much of an issue."

"I should hope not. Isn't Luis helping you these days?" her mother asked.

"Yes, he is. And *you* knew that." Stacy turned the words back against her mom. They both laughed.

"He's a good man," her mother said.

Surprised, Stacy stopped and leaned a hip against her desk. "Really? You think so?"

"I do. I'll admit when you first told me you'd found him again, I was skeptical," her mother said. "And after what I went through with your father, I think I had every right to be. But from the happiness in your voice and what you've told me about how close he and Miguel are, I think he's proved himself."

Her mom was right. Luis did make her happy. And he'd been nothing but kind and loyal and trustworthy the past few weeks. He had proven himself many times over.

The last of the barriers around Stacy's heart crumbled to dust, and in their place blossomed love. Deep, abiding, undeniable love. She'd been so scared, put it off for so long, waiting, watching.

But finally, she admitted to herself that yes. She loved Luis Durand.

And if he asked her again to be with him, she would.

Nervous butterflies took flight in her stomach. Was that what tonight was about?

He'd been a bit evasive when he'd invited her the other day, only telling her to dress nicely and to bring Miguel's favorite toys along.

"Sweetheart?" her mother said. "Are you still there?"

"Uh, yeah." Stacy straightened and finished clearing the clutter from her desk. "I'm sorry."

"I said I'd keep that Luis around. At least until I get back to Key West, then I'll want my grandson to myself for a while." Her mom chuckled.

"Right. Sure," she said, fiddling with her ponytail with her free hand, distracted.

She'd nearly conquered that niggle of

doubt inside her that warned disaster was just around the corner and Luis would walk away again, run to some far-off land and leave her and Miguel behind, just like her father had. Most days, she didn't even think about it anymore, staying busy with work on her shifts and Miguel during her time off. Then there were the hours in bed with Luis, when she let go completely and just savored her time with him, touching, kissing, holding one another, talking about anything and everything. Those were the times when she imagined a future with them together, raising their son, having more babies, living a good life in Key West. Even if that house of his made her feel like a country church mouse at a high-society wedding.

The fire station alarm went off, signaling another emergency run. Damn. "I need to go, Mom. I'll talk to you tomorrow. Love you!"

"Love you, too, honey. Good luck tonight. Kiss Miguel for me."

"I will." Stacy ended the call then rushed out to the equipment room to suit up with the rest of her crew. "What do we have?"

"Ambulance call. MVA. Mother and baby inside with injuries," one of her crew called while she finished grabbing her gear. "Aren't you about done, Captain?"

"Last run for this shift," she said, sliding into the truck just before they pulled out of the station, lights and sirens blazing.

The ride to the scene was short, as it was only about a mile away, and Stacy surveyed the wreck while the rest of her crew got out. Police were already on scene directing traffic, but the EMTs hadn't arrived yet. Not uncommon and why fire responded, too. Most firefighters cross-trained as paramedics so they could respond in emergencies. The extra boost in pay didn't hurt, either.

Stacy climbed out of the rig last and walked over to the SUV that was resting on its side. From what she could see, the other car had T-boned it, tipping the SUV over and sending it skidding into the opposite lane of traffic. The windows had shattered on impact, and the airbags had deployed. One of her crew was talking to the female crash victim in the front seat now, who seemed alert, if understandably panicked. In the background, the tiny, high-pitched wail of an infant could be heard from the rear of the vehicle, and Stacy's heart squeezed in response.

"What's the situation?" she asked, walking over to get a better look inside the wreckage. She stooped down to peer through the spiderweb of cracked glass and spotted the car seat, still strapped in tight, holding the squalling baby safely within its padded confines. The tension inside her eased slightly. She carefully knocked on the glass and cooed to the infant inside. "It's okay, little one. We're going to get you out of there, I promise."

"Is my baby okay?" the woman called from the front of the car, the seat belt cutting painfully across her clavicle, from what Stacy could tell. "Please, help my baby."

"Your baby looks fine," Stacy said, straightening and moving to the mother. The woman looked young, maybe twenty-two, twenty-three, with dark hair and light blue eyes. There was a cut on her forehead that was bleeding profusely and most likely a broken collarbone from that seat belt, but otherwise she seemed all right. They'd transport them both to the nearest hospital to be on the safe side, regardless. "We're just waiting on the ambulance to get here before we get you both out of there." In the distance more sirens wailed, and Stacy patted the woman's hand. "Sounds like that's them coming now."

"Oh, thank God," the woman said, and sure enough, minutes later, the EMTs and fire crew had both mom and baby out of the vehicle and onto stretchers with neck braces in place for transport to Key West General.

Stacy and her crew left the accident scene and headed back to the station house. It was going on 5:00 p.m. now, and she needed to get home to change then pick up Miguel from her neighbor, who was watching him this afternoon, since both she and Luis had had to work. Luis was sending a car to get them at seven for dinner at his place.

Fresh adrenaline fizzed in her blood at the thought. They'd been together for a few weeks now, and things were going well. He was everything she'd ever wanted in a man— smart, strong, kind, supportive—and he was wonderful with Miguel. The boy loved his father already, and each day they spent together only tightened the bond they shared.

It was both amazing and terrifying.

As a little girl, Stacy had thought her father hung the moon and stars. She could still remember the nights he'd sit with her and read to her or tell her stories about princesses and knights in shining armor. She'd thought her daddy would always be there. She'd been wrong.

"He's a good man. He's proved himself."
Her mother's words rang through her mind

again as Stacy stared at her reflection in the mirror a short while later. She'd chosen a dark green sheath dress to wear tonight, with matching flats. It was dressy without being too fancy and she hoped it was enough for Luis. He always looked perfect, no matter what he wore, with his handsome face and fit body. Sometimes she felt a bit dumpy, with her sensible clothes and curvy shape.

And his house…

Lord, it made her little apartment look like a shoebox. Three stories, all glass and steel and modern luxury. He even had a second house outside for guests. She'd been afraid to touch anything the first time they'd been there in case she broke something. But Luis had been so proud, and so she tried to make herself comfortable there for his sake. But Stacy had grown up lower middle class, and she never forgot her roots.

"Mommy," Miguel called from down the hall. "Do I look okay?"

She walked into his room to find him dressed like a little clone of Luis, in dark pants and a white button-down shirt. Like father, like son. She stood behind him at the full-length mirror and adjusted his collar then bent to kiss the top of his head. "You look very handsome, honey."

Miguel blushed and squirmed under her hands on his shoulders. "Mom…"

"Fine." She chuckled and ruffled his dark curls. "You look like Daddy. How about that?"

"Okay." He grinned up at her. "Is it time to go?"

Stacy checked her watch then nodded. "Just about. Let me grab my purse and then we can go downstairs to wait for the car."

The ride to Luis's house, in the exclusive community of Casa Marina on Flagler Drive, was short. They entered the property through the front gate in the whitewashed walls surrounding the compound and drove up the drive to stop beneath a portico. The style of architecture was midcentury modern, Luis had told her the first time she'd been here, and he'd designed it himself. His pride in the work was evident in his sparkling dark eyes. The driver got out and opened the door for her and Miguel, and they climbed from the back seat and walked to the door, where Luis was waiting for them, looking breathtakingly gorgeous in a suit and tie. He smiled widely at her and bent to pick up Miguel, kissing the top of the little boy's head before putting him down to let him scamper into the house and run wild.

"Hey," Luis said, bending to kiss her. This close, she could see the faint lines of stress at the corners of his eyes and around his mouth, and for a moment that tiny niggle of worry burrowed into her gut before she could stop it. Then she pushed it aside. Her mother was right. Luis was a good man. He'd more than proved himself. He wasn't like her father. He would be here for her and Miguel. Given how hard they'd both been working the past week or so, Luis was probably just tired. Still, when she pulled back, she whispered, "Everything okay?"

He smiled and ushered her inside, his hand at the small of her back sending a warm tingle of awareness through her. "Come, let me get you some wine. Dinner is almost ready."

The interior of the house was just as stunning as she remembered, all open spaces and lots of windows. The inlaid marble floors were two-tone, white around the edges with darker gray in the middle, and the furniture was all oversize and comfy-looking, in shades of ivory and taupe with brighter green and turquoise accents. Luis had mentioned his home had even been featured in *Architectural Digest* earlier in the year, and she could see why.

It was stunning, just like him.

"Please, have a seat," he said, settling her on a large sofa in the living room before going to check on Miguel in the next room, where he'd already spread out his blocks and was busy building something. Stacy could see him through the door, and the picture of father and son together, heads bent as they worked together, warmed her heart.

A few minutes later, Luis returned with a glass of chardonnay for her and a deep ruby-red cabernet for himself. They chatted for a while about their days and about Miguel, then Stacy said, "Oh, and I talked to my mom this afternoon before I left work."

"Hmm." He watched her over the rim of his wineglass, seeming a bit distracted. "How is she doing?"

"Good. In fact, she's planning on staying up in Miami for a while longer with her friend."

Luis nodded, frowning down into his wineglass. "The friend is recovering well, I hope?"

"Yes. So well, in fact, he and my mother are planning a trip to Bermuda together soon." Stacy chuckled, her pulse pounding. "Guess love finds you when you least expect it."

"Yes, it does." Luis looked up at her then,

his expression serious. "Listen, *mi sirenita*. There is something we need to discuss tonight and—"

"Mommy!" Miguel ran in to climb up on the sofa onto her lap. Luckily, Stacy moved her hand out of the way fast to avoid spilling her wine. "I'm hungry. When are we going to eat?"

She looked over at Luis, stomach nosediving to her toes. He wanted to talk. About what? Was her intuition correct for once? Was he going to ask her to take the next step with him in their relationship? "Uh, I don't know. Daddy?"

"How about now?" Luis said, setting his empty glass on the coffee table, not meeting her gaze. He stood and headed over to the open kitchen, from where the delicious scents of roasted vegetables and chicken drifted. "Just give me a moment to get everything ready to serve."

"Here." Stacy set Miguel on the seat beside hers and stood, carrying both their wineglasses to the kitchen and setting them gently in the sink. "Let me help you."

"Thanks," Luis said to her over his shoulder as he pulled a pan out of the oven. "If you could set the table, that would be great. Everything is on the island there."

"Sure." Stacy did as he asked, keeping one eye on Miguel as she did so. He'd become fascinated with the various sculptures around the living room, staring up at them like they were aliens or something. If she and Miguel did end up moving in here, those statues would have to go or risk becoming casualties of an overactive four-year-old boy. She finished setting out the plates and silverware and napkins then returned to the kitchen. Standing shoulder to shoulder with Luis at the granite island, she whispered, "What did you want to talk to me about?"

"Not now," he said, dishing up yummy-looking roasted chicken and veggies into a serving dish. "Let's have a nice meal first."

Her gut twisted a little at that. If the talk was indeed about them moving in together, then that would be a happy thing and would endanger their "nice" meal, would it? Unless he was worried about her saying no again. Maybe that was it. Frowning, she carried the serving dish into the dining room area and set it atop the long, thick glass table. It reminded her of the fancy dinners she'd seen on the telenovelas her mom used to watch on TV. Fancy people eating fancy food in fancy clothes. Considering what she and Luis were wearing, maybe they were getting posh all of a sudden.

Chuckling, she corralled her son into the dining room and got him set up in one of the chairs, then pulled it closer to her own at the end of the table so she could keep an eye on him while Luis finished bringing the salad and bread to the table. They both sat down and he poured her more wine and then they were eating. The food tasted every bit as good as it looked, and even picky eater Miguel cleaned his plate. Then he was off to play with his blocks again while she and Luis finished their wine at the table.

"So, that was very good. I didn't know you were such a good cook," Stacy said, hoping to ease that stress in his face that had only seemed to worsen through dinner. "Where did you learn to make such wonderful things?"

"During my mission trips," he said, wiping his mouth with his napkin. "On my days off, I always tried to experience the local culture as much as I could, and what better way to do that then through their food? I leaned to make dishes directly from the people in the villages I was there to help. A good exchange, I think."

"Agreed."

Awkward silence descended as she stared down at her empty plate and Luis looked anywhere but at her. Finally, he reached over and covered her hand with his. "Stacy, I got a phone call today while I was at the ER."

All the elation that had been swelling inside her like a balloon over the possibility of this being it—the moment he proclaimed his love and asked her to be his—deflated like a pricked balloon.

"Oh," she managed to say around her constricted throat, swallowing more wine to dislodge the lump now present there. "From who?"

"An old friend, Xavier Lewis. He runs the charity I used to work with, Docs on Duty."

And that lump became a boulder, crashing down into her stomach and leaving a gaping hole of shadows behind it. No. No, no, no. This could not be happening. She wanted to plug her ears with her fingers and make noise so she couldn't hear him, wanted to get up and run away. But she sat, silent and stony as he continued talking.

"I don't know if you've had a chance to watch much of the news this week, but Central America, and Honduras in particular, was hard hit with a category five hurricane a few days ago. Xavier and his team are there now, and it's bad, *mi sirenita*." He rubbed his thumb over her skin absently, his gaze far off and cloudy as he seemed to be remembering other times, other disasters. Deep down, she knew what was coming, and yet it still broke her when he said it. "He called because he needs my help. Desperately. I told him I would need to talk to you first before I agreed."

Stacy swallowed hard, her mouth dry and her eyes stinging. Of course he would run off to the rescue, because that's what Luis did. He was a good man. The best. Except where did that leave her and Miguel? Right back where they started. "I see," she croaked out, slipping her hand from beneath his. "How long will you be gone?"

Luis scowled, closing his eyes a moment. "I haven't said I'd go yet, but if I do, it would probably be for at least a month, maybe longer, depending on the conditions. Xavier said that in addition to the storm damage and flooding, they've got a serious risk of landslides from additional rains sweeping through the area."

Oh God.

Bile rose in her throat, and she gulped more wine to keep her dinner down. So, not only would she lose Luis, the man she'd fallen in love with against her better judgment and let into both her heart and her son's life, but there was a good possibility Luis could die as well.

She closed her eyes and inhaled deep through her nose. Stupid Stacy. So, so stupid. She knew better than to believe that fairy tales came true and life worked out happily ever after. She didn't begrudge Luis his charity work—in fact, she admired it. She just wished it didn't cost her everything she'd ever wanted. A home, stability, the security of knowing that someone would be there for her and Miguel no matter what at the end of the day.

"*Mi sirenita,*" Luis said, reaching over to cup her cheek. "Please. Stacy. Please say something. Talk to me. I won't go if you don't want me to. I just—"

"Just what?" She turned to him, shaking off his touch, hurt and anger pushing her to her feet, the anger mainly directed at herself for becoming so dependent on Luis. "Look, go if you want to. I need to get home because I need to figure out childcare for Miguel since you'll be gone. If you can let me know your itinerary once you get it, so I can schedule appropriately around it, I'd appreciate it." She put her napkin down and started toward the next room where her son was playing. "Come on, Miguel. Time to go home."

"Stacy, wait." Luis stood as well, following after her and taking her arm. "Please, let's discuss this. It doesn't have to change anything between us. I'll be gone a few weeks, a month at most, then we can pick up where we left off here."

"Can we?" She whirled to face him, tears welling in her eyes against her wishes. "And what about the next time, Luis? And the time after that? Because there's always going to be some dangerous disaster somewhere in the world that you're going to want to race off to. And what—Miguel and I are just supposed to sit at home and wait for you to come back? We're supposed to put our lives on hold while you keep doing things for everyone but yourself?"

She shook her head and pulled away, forcing a smile for Miguel, who was watching them closely now. "I'm sorry, but I can't do that. I know what it's like not to be enough. Hell, I've lived that my whole life, and I will not put my son through that. I won't. We won't be second best to your need to save the world. If that's what you want, fine. Go. Be a superhero. But we won't be waiting for you when you get back. I just can't do that. I'm sorry."

She walked over and helped Miguel put his blocks back into the carry case, then took his hand and headed for the front door, where the car and driver were still waiting beneath the portico. Apparently, the guy had nothing better to do in life. Good for him. Good for her, too. She charged outside, Miguel by her side, and helped her son into the back seat as the driver held the door for them.

"Stacy, please." Luis rushed outside to stand behind her. "*Mi sirenita*, don't do this. I thought we were building something strong between us. Don't tear that all down over one more mission trip."

Cheeks damp and broken heart thudding painfully against her rib cage, Stacy said, "It's not just one more, though, is it Luis? There'll always be another. And another. And what if you die over there, huh? What am I supposed to do then? How do I tell Miguel that the father he loves and just found is gone again and he's never coming back?"

Stacy lost it then, tears flowing freely now. "I'm sorry, Luis. I can't. I just can't. I already lost one man I loved. I won't sit by and do it again. Goodbye. You can say goodbye to

Miguel tomorrow at my apartment when you come by to watch him."

With that, she climbed into the car beside her son and closed the door, leaving Luis behind in the drive to watch them go, his face growing smaller and smaller in the rear window until they turned the corner and he disappeared completely.

"Mommy?" Miguel asked from beside her as she did her best to keep her sobs inside. "Are you okay?"

"No, honey, I'm not." She pulled Miguel into her side and put her head back against the seat as he hugged her tight. "But I will be tomorrow. We'll be fine."

Somehow, some way, she had to keep going. Alone.

Even if her battered heart might never heal again.

That had gone worse than Luis had expected. And it was all his fault.

He stood in the drive, watching the woman he loved leave his life, until the red taillights of the car disappeared from sight, then he went back inside. Cleaned up dinner to keep himself busy, then took off his suit coat and loosened his tie before slumping down on the sofa with another glass of wine in his hand.

He wasn't on call, so no need to worry about staying sober.

If only the alcohol could ease the pain in his heart.

God, what a mess he'd made of things tonight. He'd hoped to explain it to her gently, get her to see that it wasn't a big deal. They'd both been working so much that they hadn't seen each other a lot over the last week or so anyway. Him going to Honduras would just be like an extended period of that for a few extra weeks, and then they'd be back to normal again.

He would come back. He'd always come back to her and Miguel. Always.

And what if you die over there?

Her question returned to haunt him, and he drained his glass in one long swallow before pouring more. It was a good cabernet. Dark and deep, just like the hole he'd dug for himself.

Honestly, he'd never really considered that part of things before. He'd just gone, driven to fulfill the vow he'd made to his parents so long ago. Determined to make his life count, to honor the sacrifices they'd made so he could be here today.

But when would it be enough? When would he be allowed to rest and have a life of his own choosing? When would he have repaid his debt?

He drank his second glass of wine and poured a third, staring across the living room and out through the windows to the lush tropical gardens beyond. He was tired, exhausted, after years of giving, giving, giving. And there was still so much more to be done.

Luis conceded, reluctantly, that Stacy was right. It wouldn't be just this mission if he went back. Because there would always be more storms, more earthquakes, more impoverished areas that needed help. He could do what he could, but it would never, ever be enough.

Sinking back into the plush sofa cushions, he stared up at the ceiling, Stacy's tearstained face flashing before his eyes like a tragic movie. He hadn't even gotten to say goodbye to Miguel.

Miguel. My son. *Mijito.*

If he lost his relationship with his son because of some damned fool trip halfway around the world, that would be a tragedy indeed. He'd only known Miguel a few weeks, but he loved the boy more than his own life. He'd do anything for his son. Would do anything for Stacy, too.

Mi sirenita. My mermaid. He'd thought of

her that way since their first night together on the beach.

He loved Stacy, too, more than any other woman ever. His beautiful, strong, stubborn siren.

But can I stay?

Chest aching, he shook his head and stood again, restless and weary. There were no easy answers.

He felt stretched in two different directions and near to snapping. Usually, Luis was the person everyone else came to with their problems, and he solved them. But now he needed help, and there wasn't anyone to turn to. Jackson had his own problems going on, though he'd yet to share them with Luis. His brother was driving himself into the ground, constantly working and taking extra shifts as if the devil himself was on his tail.

Luis knew the feeling.

Maybe he'd head down to the Duck Bill Pub soon and talk to his father about things. His dad always seemed to know best, and Lord knew Luis needed some good advice.

CHAPTER TWELVE

"It's over, Mom," Stacy said on the phone. "Done. He's going off to Honduras, and Miguel and I are getting on with our lives."

"Oh, honey," her mother said. "I'm so sorry."

"Me, too." It had been six days since the dinner at Luis's house, and each time Stacy thought about that night, she really thought she ought to feel better about her actions than she did. In truth, she felt horrid. She hadn't slept more than a few hours all week, despite pulling extra shifts to cover several guys who were off sick. Yet each time she lay down and closed her eyes, all she could see was Luis's face as he'd pleaded with her to understand, the sadness in his eyes, the empty, hollow feeling where her heart used to be. She'd figured she'd cried herself out by now, but damn if fresh tears didn't sting her eyes now. "I love him, Mom. And he's gone. Just like Daddy."

"No, sweetie. Oh God. Is that what this is all about?" Her mother shushed her and murmured soothing words until Stacy got a grip on herself again. Her poor mom was always good at cheering other people up, but Stacy doubted now if she'd ever find her joy again. Silence echoed for a few moments on the phone line before her mother continued, after a huge sigh. "Well, I guess maybe that is what you got from that business with your father. But you should know, honey, that him leaving was the best thing that ever happened to us."

"What?" Surprise jolted Stacy straight out of sadness into astonishment. "How can you say that, Mom? After he left you had to work your tail off to keep a roof over our heads."

"True. But without him constantly nagging and putting me down, I got my self-esteem back. And hard work never hurt anyone." Her mother's tone turned defensive. "We always had enough, didn't we?"

"Yes, barely."

"Enough is enough. No need for more. And being on my own, with you to take care of, made me work harder."

Stacy's chest constricted at the long, horrible pause that followed. "He just left us. Walked out and never returned. I never want Miguel to have to go through that. I have to protect him. This isn't just about me."

"This is everything to do with you," her mother countered, her tone exasperated. "Listen to me, honey. You were very little when your father left, but we were both so young when we had you. Neither of us knew what we were doing, and yes, we married for all the wrong reasons. I'm sorry that him leaving and us fighting beforehand is all you remember, honey, but there were good times, too. And yes, I cried, but…"

Her mother's voice turned rough with emotion, and Stacy sat up from where she'd been lying on her sofa, devouring yet another pint of ice cream, same as she'd done each night after putting Miguel to bed since the breakup with Luis. She should buy stock in the dairy company that made these. She'd be a rich woman soon. She set her food and spoon aside and tucked her knees beneath her chin, sensing this was important. "What about the tears, Mom?"

"Not all of them are bad." Her mother sniffled and gave a little laugh. "Sometimes they can be cleansing, cathartic, too. Sometimes, they help clear away the dirt of what's been and show you a new path forward."

Stacy considered that a moment, then took a deep breath. Maybe her mother was right. Maybe she and Luis had needed to have that fight, have that pain of separation to figure out where they wanted to go from here.

"Without your dad leaving, hard as that was, I never would've put myself through school, never would've gotten my master's degree and moved up into upper management at the insurance firm. Yes, it was hard, but I wouldn't have changed it for the world." She sighed. "My only regret is that it took time away from you. And obviously left you thinking things that weren't right. My commitment to bettering our lives meant I had to work long hours and crazy shifts for a while. But after everyone told me I'd ruined my life and my chance at anything good by getting pregnant and married so young, I had to prove them wrong, honey. I wanted to show the world that I could make it on my own." Her mother chuckled. "Where do you think your stubbornness comes from, eh?"

"So, Daddy leaving was all…okay?" Stacy asked, confused and more than a little stunned.

"No. He should have said goodbye to

you, but he had problems of his own and he needed to deal with them to be any good to anyone, let alone a child. I know that hurt you, honey, but it really was for the best. You saw my tears, heard our arguments. Those came from both of us being so tired and young and jealous and guilty. He had his own path to follow and we had ours. And I think you and I did just fine for ourselves."

Stacy was crying again by the time her mom finished. "Oh God. You're right. We did do fine. But I said some awful things to Luis and didn't even give him a chance to explain himself the other night, only thought the worst of him even though he's the best man I've ever met, Mom. Seriously. He loves Miguel and he takes care of us. He takes care of everyone. And I just turned my back on him." She dropped her head onto her forearms and sobbed. "I've ruined everything. I'm so stupid."

"You are not stupid!" Her mother's fierce words jarred Stacy out of her sorrow for a minute, and she snapped her head up once more. "And don't ever talk about yourself like that again, young lady. You are smart and talented and funny and kind. You have a good heart and a smart brain. You're the mother of my grandson, who's the most perfect child ever born. And if Luis is half the man I think he is and you say he is, he'll forgive you. It may take a little work, but the best things in life often do. Now pick yourself up off that sofa and stop stuffing your feelings down with sugar and deal with it."

Abashed, Stacy quickly hid her empty ice cream carton and spoon, the wiped the double fudge remnants off the corners of her mouth with her sweatshirt sleeve. Her messy hair was piled atop her head, and she needed a good scrub. She'd done the bare minimum this past week, taking time off from the fire department to watch Miguel and wallow in her grief over losing Luis. She hadn't answered her phone or gone outside in days.

Now, though, something inside her had changed, or shifted, or both.

For the first time since their awful fight, Stacy felt a glimmer of hope. Hope that perhaps if she got her act together and put the past in the past and groveled enough, she might just be able to win Luis back.

It would take a lot of patience and care and love, but she was willing to try.

"I lost her," Luis said, sitting at the bar of an empty Duck Bill Pub.

He'd finally made it in to see his father,

though it was days later than he'd planned. Days where he'd spent nearly every waking hour at the hospital because it was easier than sitting at home in his empty house, replaying that fight with Stacy over and over again in his head. Missing Miguel, missing Stacy, missing everything he'd found during those precious weeks with them.

Family, faith, a future he wanted more than he wanted his next breath.

There'd been so many times where he'd almost charged over to her apartment and pounded on her door, demanded she see him, talk to him, let him try to work this out between them, but he'd stopped himself. Stacy wouldn't respond well to force. She deserved consideration, patience, care.

He toyed with his glass of seltzer water, frowning. He'd never been much of a drinker, since alcohol basically went straight to his head and made him sleepy. He also didn't like the way it made him feel, out of control and reckless. Take that night on the beach five years ago. He'd been drunk then and look what happened. Or the night of the dinner with Stacy. He'd finished off that bottle of cabernet after she'd gone and woken up with hell's own hangover the next morning.

And he'd then had to pull an all-nighter at work. Not good. Not good at all.

His father finished chopping up fruit for the garnishes and glanced up at him. "This the woman you were in here with a few weeks back?"

"Yeah." Luis rubbed the back of his neck. That had been the night Stacy had told him about Miguel. The night she'd changed his life forever. He wished now he could go back to then, start over again, do better. Be better.

"She's a firefighter," his dad said.

"Yep."

"I recognize her from her crew. They come in here sometimes for dinner. Good group."

Luis had thought he'd seen Stacy a few times over the past six days, and he'd perked up each time a new emergency run came in or fire truck passed, thinking he might catch a glimpse of her, but no. She'd been nowhere around, and damn. He missed her. So much it physically hurt. Missed talking to her. Missed laughing with her. Missed holding her and kissing her and sleeping with her and waking up next to her. Missed taking care of Miguel with her and even missed doing dishes with her.

He had it bad and that wasn't good, because Stacy wanted nothing more to do with him.

His phone buzzed in his pocket, but he ignored it. Most likely it was Xavier again, and he still hadn't made up his mind about that mission. Part of him said he should just go, get out of Key West for a while and help some people along the way. And if a mountain of mud slid down and buried him, well, it couldn't be any worse than what he was going through right now.

His father kept working, quietly. Too quietly.

"I came here for advice, Dad," Luis said at last, scrubbing a hand over his face. His stubble felt rough against his palm, and he probably looked as scruffy as he felt. He hadn't even bothered to change out of his scrubs after his last shift, just headed over here to hang his head and brood. "You've always been there for me since I was six years old and you and Mom took me in. I don't know what to do." He sighed and stared down into his seltzer water like the answers he sought might be in there. "I thought I was living my life in the way I should. All I ever wanted to do was make my birth parents proud. Make you and Mom proud. But I don't feel like I'm doing anyone any favors now."

Footsteps echoed behind the bar followed by the squeak of the little door that led out into the restaurant as his dad came to sit next to him.

"Let me get this straight, son," his dad said. "You and this firefighter lady have feelings for each other, but you had a fight and now she won't see you. Is that it?"

He hadn't told them about Miguel, not yet. It still hurt too much, and he and Stacy had never gotten around to discussing exactly how they were going to break that news to everyone. So he just nodded.

"Right." One of the few patrons in the place walked over to the jukebox along the wall and slid in a few quarters. The overhead speakers crackled, and a song began. Some new country tune. His father shook his head. "Thank God it isn't 'Wind Beneath My Wings' again. Since the storm, people think that's funny to play. I've heard it so many times I think my head's going to explode."

Luis managed a little chuckle at that.

"Seriously, though. Let me start off by saying your mother and I *are* proud of you, son. Always have been, always will be. You and Jackson are the best things that ever happened to Juanita and me. And as far as your birth parents? Kid, they'd be proud of you no matter what. You could sweep streets or race cars or whatever you chose to do. As long as it made you happy. That's all they ever wanted for you. Just to be happy and have the freedom to live the life you want."

After a grunt, Luis scowled. "They died bringing me here to this country. That kind of sacrifice demands greatness."

"And you don't think saving lives in your ER is greatness?" His dad gave him a side glance. "Not sure I can think of anything more heroic, son."

"It's not enough."

"Not enough?" His father snorted. "Wait a second. Is that why you spent years racing around the globe to one hot spot after another? You were trying to repay some kind of debt to them?"

It didn't sound quite so noble when his dad put it that way, but still Luis gave a curt nod.

"I see." His father inhaled deep then let it out slow, a sure sign a lecture was coming. "Okay. Well, first off, let me tell you how ridiculous that is." Luis started to object, but his dad held up a hand to stop him. "Now before you get all upset about it, hear me out. I never met your parents, that's true. But being first-generation Cuban myself, I know from whence they came. And I can tell you that the only reason any of us escaped that repressive regime was freedom, pure and simple. And that word meant different things to everyone, but it came down to being able to do what you want, when you want, in whatever way you want. For yourself and for your family. Your parents took that dangerous trip in the middle of the night through rough waters because they wanted you to be happy, Luis. That's all. There was no debt to repay, no obligation you had to fulfill attached to it. They wanted you to make a life for yourself of your choosing, to have love and a family of your own someday. That's all they ever wanted. And if you can do that, then you will have fulfilled whatever promise you made to them."

It took a moment for those words to sink into his mind, really sink in, but when they did, Luis felt like a huge burden had been lifted off his shoulders, one he'd been carrying his whole life without realizing it. He raised his head and looked at his father. "You really think so?"

"Son, I know so," his dad said, grinning. "Is that the advice you needed?"

"I think so." Luis downed the rest of his seltzer water in one gulp, feeling more energetic and hopeful than he had in days. He knew what he needed to do nnow. All he had to figure out was how to go about it. "Thanks, Dad. I've got to go. There are some things I need to take care of."

"Sure, sure," his father said, picking up his towel again and slinging it over his shoulder. As Miguel crossed the threshold out onto sunny Duval Street, his dad called from behind him. "And if you see that brother of yours, tell Jackson to call me. Haven't heard from him in a while, either."

CHAPTER THIRTEEN

STACY TOOK A deep breath and stared at herself in the mirror on the wall of her office at the fire station. After the conversation with her mother yesterday, she knew she needed to find a way to talk to Luis again and apologize for how she'd reacted to his news, but she was still figuring out what to say.

Frankly, she was shaken. Finding out that all the things she'd thought about her parents' breakup all these years weren't true had left her reeling. If she'd been so off about that, what other things had she gotten wrong?

Luis, for one.

Yep. No way around that. She'd screwed up with him big-time. The one man she should've let into her heart and she'd stonewalled him. Well, no more. For what felt like the first time in forever, she was open. Open and raw and vulnerable, and it was scary as hell. Also exhilarating, but also frightening.

What if he couldn't forgive her? What if he decided she and Miguel were more trouble than they were worth and left Key West permanently? What if she lost him all over again when she'd only just finally found him?

All the turmoil left her throat tight and her stomach churning. Of course, it didn't help that the fire chief wanted to see her in his office, either. The last thing she was focused on at this point was work, but she needed to pull it together. If she and Miguel were going to be on their own from now on, she needed her job more than ever.

After a deep breath to steady and center herself, Stacy adjusted her white uniform shirt and smoothed a hand down her black pants, then headed out into the hall toward her boss's office. She passed several of her crew along the way, and they gave her encouraging nods or smiles. Seemed the gossip mill around here was alive and well, which was another reason why she hadn't told anyone about her and Luis. A good thing, she supposed, since it could all be over.

Her heart squeezed painfully at that, and she resisted the urge to rub her chest over the sore spot, instead raising her hand to knock on the fire chief's door.

There seemed to be fewer people around the station house today for some reason. Even the chief's secretary wasn't at her desk. But it had been slow today, and maybe people were taking time off after the storm to rest and recharge, she supposed.

"Come in, AC Williams," a low, masculine voice said. When she entered, he waved her into a chair in front of his desk while he finished up a phone call. "Yes. Fine. Thank you, Mayor. I'll get right on it."

Chief Hernandez ended the call then smiled across the desk at Stacy. "Thanks for taking time out of your busy day to speak with me."

"Of course," Stacy said, swallowing hard against the arid desert that had formed in her mouth. "What did you want to see me about, sir?"

"First off, let me commend you and your crew on a job well done during Hurricane Mathilda and the subsequent cleanup. I'm meeting with all my ACs to pass on my well wishes to the rest of the department."

Stacy gave a small nod. "I'll be sure to let them know. They'll appreciate it, I'm certain."

"Good." The chief clasped his hands atop his desk. A bulky man, he was in his mid-fifties, with thick salt-and-pepper hair and a handlebar moustache. "Moving on to my second order of business then. I'm sure you've heard Battalion Chief Webber is retiring next month?"

"Uh…" Stacy blinked at him. She'd vaguely heard something about it a few weeks ago, but what with the storm and all, it had fallen off her radar. "His wife was sick, I think?"

"Yes. Breast cancer. But she beat it, thank God." Hernandez raised his hands skyward for a second then zeroed his attention in on her again. "Webber understandably wants to spend more time at home, enjoy life again, reconnect with his wife, so I'm considering candidates to fill his position. You're at the top of my list, Captain Williams."

"Oh." Stunned, she just sat there a second, wide-eyed. Of all the things she thought this meeting could have been about, that wasn't it. "Um, wow. I don't know what to say, sir. Thank you for considering me."

"You check all the boxes. You're smart, ambitious, hardworking, knowledgeable, and all your crew members speak very highly of your leadership skills."

Huh. That explained the nods and smiles she'd gotten over the past few days, then.

"There's an increase in rank, of course,

but also a substantial raise in pay as well," the chief continued. "Webber's planning on retiring next month, so I'd like to get someone into the position as soon as possible to make the transition a smooth one. You'd be overseeing not just the fire stations here on Key West but throughout the other Keys as well, and you'd report directly to Assistant Chief Mercer. Sound like something you'd be interested in?"

It was what she'd worked for since she'd transferred to Key West, honestly. She'd just never expected it to happen so quickly. Then again, a lot of things in her life had happened fast—meeting Luis at that party, getting pregnant with Miguel, suddenly finding Luis again after five years apart. Overall, those quick changes had been good things. Given her situation, she'd be a fool to turn it down. But she needed to talk with Luis first. It was only fair, since he'd talked to her about the Honduras mission trip, even if she'd handled it badly.

She owed him that. Owed him so much more, truthfully.

And it was debt she hoped she'd get a chance to repay a millionfold in the future.

"I'm flattered to be your top pick, sir. Really. But could I have a few days to think it over?" she asked, hands clenched in her lap to hide their tremble. Excitement and astonishment and anxiety sizzled through her in an intoxicating mix. "There's someone I need to discuss it with first."

"Ah, of course, Captain Williams." Chief Hernandez grinned. "Absolutely. How about we meet again on Friday and you can give me your answer then?"

"Perfect." Stacy stood and shook his hand. "Again, I really appreciate your support and confidence in me, sir. I'll speak with you again in a few days."

Stacy walked out of the office and bit back a whoop of joy. Life was funny. A few weeks ago, they'd experienced the wrath of Mathilda, with all the danger and destruction the storm brought with it. A few more weeks before that, Luis had just been a brilliant memory from her past, one she'd never expected to see again. Now, all her dreams seemed to be coming true professionally, while her personal life hung in the balance.

She walked back to her office, pulling out her phone along the way to see a text from Lucy on her screen.

Service dog ready for Miguel next week. Will call later with details.

Yep, dreams coming true all around.

Her son would have his canine companion just in time for the start of school, and if Stacy's good luck held, she might have a chance to see Luis again, too. Even if he didn't take her back, hopefully they could at least reconcile enough to keep things peaceful between them for Miguel's sake.

Miguel loved his daddy.

Stacy did, too.

So much she ached.

Please, God. Please let him forgive me. Please help us find our way past this and back to good again.

She looked up just in time to avoid colliding with Harley and Jeffrey, who were loitering by her office door, looking suspicious. "What? No fires to put out today, guys?"

"Uh, we actually just got a call, Captain," Jeffrey said, following her into the room. "Waiting on you to go."

Stacy frowned. "I didn't hear the alarm go off."

"No. It's a nonemergency run, but they requested fire backup," Harley said, filling the doorway with his muscled frame, arms crossed and expression unreadable. "We're ready when you are."

"You guys go on ahead," she said, sitting

down at her desk. "I've got some things to catch up on here before I go home to Miguel."

The two exchanged a look, then moved to flank her sides.

"No can do, Captain," Jeffrey said. He was in his early twenties and was still filling out his height, all gangly legs and long arms. At her pointed look, his cheeks reddened. "I mean, we really need you on this one, Captain."

"Why?" The adrenaline from her meeting earlier with the chief was quickly burning away to annoyance. "If it's nonessential, then you don't need a full crew. You and Harley grab a couple more people and go. I have things to do here."

Things like calling Luis and setting up a time to talk.

"Uh...there is no one else," Harley said. "I sent them all to lunch."

"All of them?" She gave her crew member an incredulous look then glanced at the clock. "It's almost three in the afternoon. A bit late for lunch, isn't it?"

"We were busy earlier." Harley shrugged. "So we need you to come with us to make up the numbers."

"Guys?" She called on the last threads

of her rapidly fraying patience. "What is going on?"

"Just come on, Captain," Jeffrey said, his tone pleading. "Please?"

Irritated and intrigued, she finally gave up and walked out of her office and out to the truck bay with them. "This better be good," she said, pulling on her gear then climbing into the back of the truck with Jeffrey. "And it better not take too long. I need to get home to Miguel before my neighbor leaves for work."

"Won't take long, Captain," Harley said, steering the big rig out of the bay and onto the street. "And it will definitely be good. Promise."

Alarm bells went off inside Stacy's head. Something was going on, but as they headed away from the station toward downtown Key West, all she could do was sit back and enjoy the ride.

Luis had been running around all morning, from one case to the next. Busy was good, especially today. It kept him from being too nervous about what he had planned.

"Any word on those blood work results for the patient in trauma bay one?" he asked one of the nurses at the desk.

"Let me check, Doc," she said, typing on her computer. "Nope. Nothing yet. Oh." The nurse reached down under the desk and pulled out a small cage, setting it on the counter near Luis. "Your abdominal pain patient we just sent up to surgery had this in his car. Asked if you would keep an eye on it for him. I've been trying to get him to eat, but I don't think he's feeling well."

Luis sighed and peered into the cage at the small turtle there, chewing on a leaf nearly twice his size. "Great. Looks like it's you and me, buddy. Can you put him in my office for me?"

"Sure thing, Doc," she said before heading off down the hall, cage in hand.

They were a bit short staffed today, so he was helping out wherever he could at this point. Luis had just started going through a stack of patient files when his brother, Jackson, arrived. His brother looked like hell, dark circles under his eyes and lines around his mouth from stress. From his dark scowl, Luis imagined Jackson probably felt like hell, too. He wanted to know why but was smart enough not to ask at this point.

"Feeling better, Mr. Regional Director?" Luis asked, staring down at his files again.

"Yeah." From his brother's gruff tone, it

sounded like the exact opposite. At Luis's arched brow, Jackson leaned his elbow on the counter. "I guess."

"Problems with the leg laceration?" Luis arched a brow as he continued jotting notes in his chart.

"Nope. Lucy did a good job fixing me up."

"Well, I'm glad someone finally did." Luis couldn't help a little snark, hoping it might cheer his brother up a bit. Didn't seem to work, however, as Jackson's dark frown stayed firmly in place.

"Uh, can we talk?" Jackson asked.

Luis stared at him for a moment, then handed his chart to the nurse behind the desk before gesturing for Jackson to follow him down the hall to his office. He had about a half an hour before his big plans got underway. Would do him good not to dwell on it, considering how nervous he was. He just hoped the fire crew got Stacy here on time or else it would all be for naught. He walked into his office and gestured toward the chairs in front of the desk without looking. "Have a seat."

Whoops. Luis turned around just in time to see the turtle cage on the chair where the nurse had left it. He gestured his brother away. "Other chair."

Jackson barely stopped himself in time then straightened and looked behind him, biting off a curse. The tiny creature blinked up at him. "Why's there a baby turtle in your office?"

Heat climbed Luis's cheeks as he thought of Stacy and Miguel again. His son would love a pet. They'd talked about it on several occasions. He knew Stacy was getting him a service dog, but maybe a turtle would be good, too. He'd have to talk to Stacy about it later, if things went well today...

"The poor thing's not feeling well," Luis said, pointing at the turtle. "We can't get him to eat."

Jackson looked at him. "We?"

"His owner is stuck in the hospital, and there was no one to care for the poor thing, so I thought Stacy and I..."

Damn. Realizing he'd said too much, Luis shut up fast. Awkward silence fell as he hoped his brother wouldn't notice, but Jackson was too sharp for that.

Jackson blinked at him a moment, and Luis knew his anticipation was written all over his face. He couldn't help it. He loved Stacy, more than any woman he'd ever loved before. And he loved Miguel, too, more than he ever thought it was possible to love another human being. He planned to tell them that today. He also planned to tell them he wasn't going anywhere.

He'd phoned Xavier back and given him the names of three other doctors who were as experienced with search and rescue or more so than Luis himself. He was tired of traveling, tired of danger and distress. He was ready to settle down and start a family, start a future with Stacy and Miguel.

If they'd still have him.

Luis glanced at the clock then sat back in his chair, shifting his attention from the growing bubble of nervous energy inside him and toward his brother across from him. He narrowed his gaze on his brother's strained expression. "You haven't been the same since you came back from Big Pine Key. Something else happened during the hurricane."

It wasn't a question.

He and Jackson had always had a special bond, and they trusted each other completely. He'd implied what was happening between himself and Stacy and hoped his brother might confide in him as well.

After a long moment, Jackson sighed and stared down at his feet. "Maybe."

Right. His brother was a secretive person,

especially about matters of the heart, so his answer spoke volumes. "I thought so." Luis gave a short laugh. "So, what are you going to do about her?"

Jackson stared at Luis a moment, as if coming to some decision, the turned to the baby turtle again. "You care if I take this little guy off your hands for a bit?"

"Why?"

"I think a vet should take a look at him."

Luis gave a lopsided smile then came around the desk to hand him the crate. "Take good care of him, brother. He belongs to my patient."

"Will do." Jackson peered inside the front of the cage, walked to the door, then turned back. "My shift's over, so I might be gone for a few—"

"Take whatever you need. My patient won't be released for a few more days."

Jackson nodded. "Thanks, brother. I owe you one."

"Yes, you do." Luis chuckled, following Jackson out into the hall then stopping to check his watch again. Five minutes. Right. He took off his lab coat and tossed it back in his office, then checked his reflection in the glass on his door as he left. His blue scrubs weren't ideal for what he planned to do, but they were who he was. Stacy knew that. He'd showered and shaved before coming in, and his curly hair was still relatively behaved. He smoothed a hand over it, then peeked into the pocket on his scrub shirt to make sure his precious cargo was still in there. Check.

"Doc, incoming," one of the nurses said from down the hall. She winked at him then left in a flurry of squeaky shoes on linoleum. "Good luck!"

Luis said a silent prayer, then headed out to the automatic doors near the ambulance bay just as a fire truck pulled up outside, horn honking and sirens wailing to announce their arrival. He walked outside into the warm day, heart pounding and blood racing. Several doctors and nurses had already gathered there, along with a couple off-duty EMTs and a good chunk of Stacy's fire crew. Even Reed and his wife were there, standing off to the side with his walker, under the shade of the portico, grinning from ear to ear.

Stacy climbed out of the back of the truck looking confused and thoroughly annoyed. She glanced around then turned back to the driver. "Harley, what the hell is going on?"

The burly guy behind the wheel walked around the truck to stand before Stacy as a second firefighter, a young guy, climbed out behind Stacy then shut the door on the rig. For a moment, Luis stood there, on the brink of everything he wanted and nothing he'd ever expected, before striding forward to Stacy.

"They brought you here for me," he said, gazing into her beautiful blue eyes. She was dressed in her gear and her hair was pulled back in a ponytail as usual, her only makeup the gloss on her lips. Luis had never seen a more gorgeous sight in his life.

She opened her mouth, then closed it, finally saying, "Hi."

"Hi," he whispered back. Part of him wanted to fall to one knee right there and beg her to be his forever, but he had some things to say first, so he swallowed hard and continued. "I asked your crew to bring you here today because I need to tell you that I love you, Stacy Williams. I've loved you since that first night on the beach, and these past few weeks with you and Miguel have been the best of my life. I've loved every minute of getting to know you and our son. I've loved making you laugh and sitting with you when you cry. I've loved getting our son ready for the day and reading to Miguel at night. But most of all, I've loved being a family with you and Miguel. Being with you both made me realize that I don't need to rush off to far-flung lands to make a difference. I can do that right here, in this hospital, in this community, with you. With Miguel. I want to do that, now and forever."

Hope and hesitation flashed in Stacy's eyes. "What about Honduras?"

"The charity is well staffed now for Honduras, or for any other disasters that might come in the foreseeable future. They don't need me anymore. I'm needed right here, with you. At least, I pray I am." He reached into the pocket of his scrubs and pulled out the small velvet box, creaking it open before kneeling on the cold cement. He took her trembling hand in his and held her teary blue gaze. "Stacy Williams, I know there is much we still need to learn about each other, but I want to be there with you every step of the way. Now, today and always. Will you marry me?"

"I…" She stared down at him, cheeks damp and pink, and he lived and died in those few seconds.

Then a voice yelled from the small crowd surrounding them, followed by a high-pitched squeal of delight. Miguel. The little boy rushed up to them, quivering with joy. "Daddy! Are you coming back? Please,

Mommy! Please can Daddy come stay with us forever?"

Stacy looked from Luis to Miguel then back again. "How did you get here?"

"Ms. Abrams brought me." Miguel pointed over to the neighbor from Stacy's apartment complex who'd been babysitting him. "She said Daddy called her this morning."

Luis shrugged up at Stacy and grinned. "I thought he should have some say in the matter, too. Since he's the one who brought us back together again."

Her blue eyes widened, and then she sniffled and knelt before him, her one hand still in Luis's and her other on Miguel's back, bringing their son closer. "I'm sorry."

His heart sank. "For what?"

"For what I said the other night. I shouldn't have made you choose like that. It wasn't fair. If your passion is helping people, then that's what you should do and I should love you and want you because of that, not despite it. And I do." She sniffled and blinked hard before meeting his gaze again. "Love you, I mean. Unconditionally. Uncontrollably. Irrevocably."

"Me, too, Daddy!" Miguel chimed in. "Irre… Irre… Irrevascably!"

Miguel bungled the word completely and

Luis couldn't have cared less. In fact, it was probably the most adorable and sweetest thing he'd ever heard.

"So," he said, his voice thick with emotion. "Will you marry me?"

His gaze darted from mother to son then back again.

Stacy gave him a watery smile then nodded. "Yes. I'll marry you."

Whoops and cheers and applause rose from the gathered crowd, drawing even more people out of the hospital to see what was going on. Luis let Stacy go to slide the ring on her finger, then pulled her and Miguel into a group hug, kissing them both on the cheek. When Miguel scampered off back to Ms. Abrams, and the crowds began dispersing, he pulled Stacy closer, cupping the back of her head, relishing the silky softness of her hair and how her soft curves molded perfectly to his hard edges. This was what he wanted. Just this, for the rest of his life. "Thank you."

Now, it was her turn to ask, "For what?"

"For everything."

She laughed. "Better hold that thought a second. I forgot to tell you that my boss offered me a battalion chief position today. It's more money, but it's also more responsibility, which means more work. Are you okay with me taking it?"

"I'm okay with it if you're okay." He smiled. "I just want you to be happy. As happy as you've made me."

"I'll think about it," she said. "Depends on how soon we plan to expand our family."

"Expand, eh?" His heart expanded in his chest to the point it was hard to breathe, and he just gathered her close, grinning. "Is that what we're going to do next?"

"Maybe," she said after a moment of holding him. "If you want to, I mean."

He drew in a deep lungful of her scent, then he felt a huge grin stretch his lips. "Oh, yes, *mi sirenita*. I want to. Very, very much."

CHAPTER FOURTEEN

One month later

THE WHOLE ERT team was gathered in the back room of the Duck Bill Pub on Duval Street to celebrate the return to readiness level one and the successful ongoing efforts at cleanup after Hurricane Mathilda. Life wasn't one hundred percent back to normal, but it was closer than before.

For Jackson and Lucy and Luis and Stacy, it was better than ever.

"I'd like to offer a toast," Luis said, standing at the front of the large room, a bottle of dark ale in his hand. "To my brother, Jackson Durand, for guiding us all through the crisis with a steady hand and a clear vision. The ambulance authority is lucky to have you as regional director."

"Hear, hear," the rest of the team cheered, clinking glasses and laughing.

"And to Dr. Luis Durand," Jackson said, hoisting his own bottle of craft beer high. "Who took over for me on short notice and kept things running properly in my absence. You run the best damned ER in Florida, man, and you're an asset to the Keys."

"And to Battalion Chief Stacy Williams," one of the firefighters said. "Congrats on the promotion!"

Another rousing cheer went up, followed by a new Jimmy Buffett tune piped in through the overhead sound system. Pretty soon people broke up into groups, dancing or talking or indulging in the excellent taco bar set up against one wall of the private room.

Jackson settled back down at his table with Lucy and rubbed her service dog Sam's side under the table with his foot. The dog went pretty much everywhere with them, as did King, Jackson's kitten, whose cage was on the seat beside him. Actually, the kitten was more cat now than anything, taller and leaner, moving fine on three legs.

Lucy reached across the table and took his hand, beaming with joy, and his heart squeezed with sweetness. Jackson was a lucky, lucky man, and he knew it. Life had given him a second chance in Lucy, and he refused to take it for granted, not for a second.

Luis and Stacy came over and sat in the chairs opposite them, holding hands and kissing, unable to keep their hands off each other. Jackson had never known his reserved brother to be so open with his public displays of affection before, but then he'd never seen Luis so in love before, either.

It was weird and wonderful, that they'd both found their soul mates during the hurricane. But considering how unconventional their childhoods had been, why should their love lives be any different?

"We have an announcement to make," Luis said, his arm around Stacy's shoulders.

"What?" Lucy asked, her fingers tightening on Jackson's. She didn't do well with surprises, and he brought her hand to his lips, kissing it, hoping to reassure her that whatever it was, they'd handle it together. "Something good, I hope?"

"We think so," Stacy said, glancing at Luis. "We're having a baby. I'm pregnant."

"Dude!" Jackson grinned. "Congratulations. That's awesome!"

"I'm so happy for you!" Lucy hugged her friend then took her seat once more, lacing her fingers with Jackson's again. "I'm going to be an aunt again."

"Yes, you are." Luis kissed Stacy then rested his head against hers. "And Miguel's going to be an older brother."

"Have you told him yet?" Jackson asked.

"Not yet," Stacy said. "You guys are the first to know, so don't tell anyone, please."

"Promise." Jackson took another sip of beer, aware of the lump in his jeans pocket. He had a secret himself, one he hoped would result in a happy announcement, too. But he had to ask Lucy first, and for that he needed a bit of privacy. So, after one more swig of alcohol for courage, he stood and looked down at the woman he loved. "Let's take a walk on the beach."

"Oh…uh…" She looked from him to Luis and Stacy. "What about Sam?"

"We can watch him for you for a second," Stacy said, winking. "Go on."

Luis held up his bottle. "Go for it, brother."

Jackson took a deep breath and led Lucy out of the pub and down the street toward the beach. Tourists were beginning to flock back to the area, but it was still not as crowded as usual, which was good, since he hoped to find a secluded spot for his special proposal.

They strolled along the sand, hand in

hand, to a spot where a few sea-swept boulders lined the shore. He helped Lucy up to take a seat on one of them, then climbed up beside her. For a long moment, they just sat side by side, watching the sunset as the sky erupted in fiery reds and oranges and deeper purples. It felt right. It felt perfect. It felt like forever.

And speaking of forever...

"Uh... Lucy," he said, moving away slightly to pull the small velvet box from his pocket. "There's something I want to ask you."

Her dark eyes widened as she looked from his hand to his eyes. "What?"

"I know it's only been a month, and I just moved in with you at the compound, but I wanted to give you something to show how much you mean to me, how invested I am in this relationship and how I plan to be around for as long as you'll have me."

"Oh God..." She covered her mouth with a shaky hand. "What are you...?"

He opened the box to reveal a sparkling diamond engagement ring. "Lucy Miller, will you marry me?"

Tears welled in her lovely eyes, and she bit her lip. "Jackson. I..." She sniffled then nodded fast. "Yes! Yes, I'll marry you. I mean, not right now. We have lots of stuff to work out first. But someday. We'll need to pick a date. Not an odd day. An even one. I'll need to look at my calendar and find out when we…"

He kissed her, as much to distract her from her tic as just because he wanted to. "I love you, Lucy. Everything about you."

She smiled through her tears and hugged him tight. "Even with my quirks?"

"Because of your quirks," he said, squeezing her tight then pulling back. "Should we go tell the others now?"

Lucy admired her ring then nodded. "Yep. Let's go make an announcement of our own."

* * * * *